Fic 18/24 £2—

The Damask Weaver

Alan Addison

Dedication

This book is dedicated to all those people who work constantly by hand and by brain to earn their pay.

Other works of fiction

Justified Sinner
Treaty of Union
Shaking Hands with a Tarantula
Finding Sophie
Working for Josh
Lullaby of the Soul
Polis & Poltergeist

Non-fiction

Using Scots in family literacy
Macnib's Legacy
Teachers notes, Scottish book trust.

Glossary

Scots language is used by a few characters in the book. If this language is not one of yours, there is a Scots-English glossary at the end of the book. You can also find Scots language dictionaries on the world wide web.

Acknowledgements

I wish to thank my dear friends Rosemary Holmes and Iain and Liz Mackie for helping turn my meagre manuscript into a work worth reading.

CHAPTER ONE
Saturday 26th December 1868

'Martha, would you see to that lass, she's howling the place down and I've got to finish this panel for the Master before the day's out.'

Martha could barely hear her husband for the noise of the handloom, nor see him for the fine flax dust that filled the air of the cottage. The only reprieve from the gloom was from the shards of daylight that sliced their way in through the tiny glass panes of the one window. 'She's only a wee girl Robert, she shouldn't be having a baby at her age. Eighteen years and no knowledge of this world. I would give that Thomas Havington what for if he didn't belong to the Big House.'

'Well he does and he'll be coming over here soon enough with their leftover dinner from yesterday. Maybe you could have a word with him then?'

As if on cue the front door opened and in strode a tall young man no more than eighteen years of age himself. He carried a woven basket and placed it on the eating table. 'Father said to bring you this.'

No-one answered until the silence between them was broken by Mary's screams.

'I must go,' he said, retreating towards the door.

'Aye, you must,' called Robert. 'You'll have the other houses to visit too.'

Thomas stopped at the door and turned. 'Pardon?'

Robert continued weaving but the young man stood his ground. When no answer was forthcoming he turned again and left.

'Where is that doctor?' shouted Robert. 'The Master said he'd send for him.'

'He'll have been held up. Dr Wemyss is a busy man and the only doctor in all of Dalgety Bay.'

'Aye, held up by his dram taking,' answered the weaver.

'Mary's mother sat down on the stool beside the bed. 'Hang on my wee darling, Doctor Wemyss won't be long.'

When the door opened they expected to see Dr Wemyss but it was William their son with his wife Christine.

'William we thought you were that bloody doctor!'

William could hardly hear his father for the clanking and banging of the hand loom. But he could hear his sister. 'You'll not be seeing that man today, he's in the North Gatehouse enjoying the Meldrum's hospitality.'

Robert stopped weaving. 'He's what?'

'We're going to have to deliver the bairn ourselves.'

'Can we put some water on the stove to boil Mrs Peterson?' asked Christine.

Martha lifted a large black metal pot from the stove and disappeared outside. When she returned she was carrying the long handle in both hands. She placed it carefully on the stove. 'It's so cold out.'

As the water began to boil Christine pulled the stool close to the bed and sat down. 'Mary, the doctor can't make it so we are going to bring your wee darling into the world. You'll have to do exactly as I tell you now Mary.'

\#

Thomas Peterson was born at 3.36pm. Any sun that had dared pierce the small window of the weaver's cottage was gone from the sky and the dark shadows of the trees that surrounded the place danced mournfully in the candlelit room.

Mary had bled profusely and the covers and cloths were bright red with her blood. 'Ye'd better get some blackpudding on the stove mother,' said Robert, 'she'll be needing iron.'

'Ye daft galoot, can ye not see the lass is exhausted. Leave her to sleep.'

'We'll get away now mother, before it gets any caulder,' said William. 'Christine will come over first thing tomorrow and see Mary is all right. You'll have enough to do looking after that yin.' He pointed to his father, who threw a wooden bobbin at him in response.

'Your aim is not what it was either father.' At that William disappeared, followed by his wife.

CHAPTER TWO
Sunday 27th December

'Martha, the Master wants me to work with the gardener today. He needs logs for the fires in the Big House. It's as well I finished that panel last night.'

'Last night? It was gone three o'clock this morning before that infernal machine stopped its wearisome noise. Mary and her bairn would have been better off sleeping in the coal yard.'

'How do you think she is?'

'She's not good Robert, but with care she should recover.'

'What about the bairn?'

'Thomas? He's going to be a fine looking man. Just like his father.'

'Aye, but without the land.'

'Now don't go on about that again. We'll have to wait a while before we see what happens to young Thomas. Do you wish a piece with you?'

'No, I should be back by mid-morning. Is there much left in that basket?'

'I've made a pot of broth with the goose bones.'

'Bones was all there was eh.'

'We had that nice bit of fruit loaf.'

'Aye, a fruit loaf that you had picked the fruit for until their cook called on it.' Robert left the cottage then and walked out into the forest to meet the gardener.

'Mary darling, your father is away at the wood cutting. I've made you a nice bowl of broth. Do you feel like sitting up a while?'

'No mother, I'll stay here.'

'You canna stay there forever Mary and Thomas will need looking after.'

Her daughter stirred and pulled herself upright. 'What's going to happen to him Ma?'

'I don't know daughter. The Master will make up his own mind what happens to the bairn and what happens to the bairn's father. He might be packed off to the army like his ancestors. Generals the lot of them.

'I love him Ma.'

'I know you do, hen, and I think he loves you too but I don't know what will come of this, for you or Thomas. My main hope is we are not asked to leave this house.'

\#

'It surely is a cauld one eh Robert?'

'It is that John.

'Did you get yon panel finished?'

'Aye, wove and delivered. But you obviously didnae cut enough logs for the Big House.'

'Nobody told me that half of Edinburgh would be staying over Christmas. They must have every fire in the house going.'

'Could they not just use their own coal from their own mines?'

'They only use that in the kitchen to give cook a better heat for her stove.' It's precious stuff Robert; most of it finds its way down to St. David's Harbour and the ships, as well you know. Yon coal will travel further than you and I ever will.'

11

Robert took hold of one end of the long saw and John, head gardener, the other. 'How are things in your cottage John?'

'It's a gie auld place but we get plenty shelter from the winds that blaw off the Forth. Yon high walls of the garden do more than protect his flowers. I do wish I could have done better for Annie. Her children away to seek their fortune and only the two of us in that draughty place. And with me at the garden from dawn till dusk it's a Godsend that your Martha comes around for the herbs and the rhubarb to make her medicines or she'd see no-one. What about your cottage Robert?'

'Much the same, but we're warm enough thanks to the wood but that dust is killing the women. And now we've the bairn too.'

'Aye, we could hear wee Mary's screams yesterday. Those screams would keep the ghosties at bay, for sure. You say the women are not getting a breath in there? I think maybe the man too. You're wheezing like the engine that takes the coal to the harbour.'

'Aye, that's as maybe.'

The saw began it long strokes backwards and forwards between the two elderly men for the best part of the morning.

\#

'Well, I must say George, you do put on a good show.'

'What better way to prepare one's father-in-law for a day's shoot than with a hearty breakfast Kenneth?' In the Big House, George William Havington, The Viscount Masterton, was standing side by side at the buffet table and addressing his father-in-law Kenneth Dalglish, The Earl Rathmore.

'And how is our little darling enjoying life North of the Forth?'

'I think she'll get used to it. Not as grand as her family seat of course but we do have the gardens and parkland to keep her occupied.'

'Our Alice has always been one for horticulture, even as a wee girl. They tell me your boy Thomas has somewhat different pursuits and has been keeping himself busy of late.'

'He must take after his mother. My first wife Elizabeth was a bit of a wild card..'

'The Matrimonial Causes Act must have saved you a pretty penny did it not. Having her packed off to the colonies after the divorce was for the best. I'm sure she'll find plenty to occupy herself with the Kaffirs?' Earl Rathmore poured himself a dram from a stone jug. 'Have you decided what's to happen to Thomas?'

George William Havington turned and looked to the servant standing by the long table. 'If you'll excuse me Kenneth, I believe I am being summoned. We've much to organize for today's shoot, not least the hampers.'

'Good show George.'

#

Christine arrived as Martha was spoon-feeding soup to her daughter.

'Chrissie, come away in, you're just in time for a wee drop soup.'

'No thank you Mrs Peterson, I've not long had my porridge. I came to see how our lass and the wee lad are faring.'

'The wee one's in fine voice, as ye can hear. This yin,' she pointed at her daughter with the spoon, 'is doing okay too. Isn't that right Mary?'

Her daughter merely nodded.

'Is there anything I can do to help,' asked Christine.

'You've done much already Chrissie by bringing Thomas into this world.'

'William and I were talking about that last night. He's a wee smasher.'

'Where is my son, I thought he'd be here helping his father? Martha knew her daughter-in-law was desperate to have children of her own but though having been married for nearly ten years there was no sign she would carry a child. 'And what were you saying last night?'

Christine's face reddened and she sat down on the same stool she'd sat on to assist in the delivery of Thomas the day before. She was looking at the floor, and not at Martha when she replied, 'William wants us to take the wee one.'

For a moment there was silence. When Christine looked up, Martha had stopped what she was doing and was looking straight at her.

'William wants you to take Mary's child. Where to? Is it for a wee visit to your home?'

'William has been offered a job weaving wire over in Leith. He says we could look after the bairn and it would prevent any problems coming down on you from the Big House.'

'That's what William said is it? Well you listen carefully to me lass. Thomas Peterson will be staying here at Fordom for the foreseeable future. I do not know what makes you think that you have the right to raise this subject but it is not one welcome in this house. Now maybe you should just take yourself away home to William and tell him from his mother that Thomas Peterson belongs in Fordom with his mother and not in that cesspit across the Forth.

'His grandfather the Viscount will not wish to have him here. This could bring trouble for you and Robert.'

'Goodbye Christine and mind how you close the door, you wouldn't want to frighten the bairn.'

'Mrs Peterson, I, we didn't mean any harm by it.'

'Be that as it may, I'd like you to leave now.'

#

It was late morning as Christine made her way back up the hill to Mossgreen, their small, rented cottage, but the dark snow clouds made it feel like late afternoon. She and William had lived at Mossgreen since their marriage ten years before.

Just as his father and grandfather before him, William had been employed as a damask weaver. The only real difference being that they worked for the Havingtons of the Big House while he, once he'd reached the age of fourteen, worked for one of the Dunfermline hand-loom producers. But the success of the Pilmuir Works with its steam looms meant that Williams's handloom job, along with that of many others, was no more.

Apart from helping his father, he now took whatever work he could find. He had, as yet, resisted going into the coal pits that belonged to the Big House. What this meant in money terms was that there was very little but he was on hand to help keep up with demand from the new Mistress for damask or wood for her fires.

But that is not where William was this morning. He had decided to go hunting. It was no wild game he was after though but the hide of Dr Wemyss.

\#

'Is Dr Wemyss at home?'

'He is that William. Is it about Mary? She'll not be long now before she has that bairn. I'll see if the doctor will see you. I won't be a moment.' The housekeeper left William standing on the front path of the Victorian pile. She was away more than ten minutes before she reappeared holding a piece of paper. 'The doctor is not feeling too well William but he has written out some instructions for Martha and Christine. He says for you to have this.' She produced a pork pie from her apron pocket and handed it to him. 'Oh and this,' she handed him a small stone bottle. 'It's a wee drop of his favourite tipple.'

William pushed passed the housekeeper and strode into the hall. 'Where is he?'

'William, Dr Wemyss is indisposed and cannot see you.'

He walked up to her. 'I'll not ask you again. Where is he?'

She pointed at a door at the end of the hall but said nothing.

'William, did Phebe not give you my note?' Dr Wemyss was sitting eating breakfast at the kitchen table.

'A bit late for breakfast Doctor. I see you like a wee dram with it too.'

'Hair of the dog. I may have overstayed my welcome with the Meldrum's last day. How is young Mary?'

'Mary had her child yesterday.'

'That is wonderful news William. Is it a boy or a girl?'

'Do you not remember that you were called upon to be at the birth?'

'As a matter of fact I do, but to be truthful I thought Mary would be a day or two yet in giving birth.'

'And how did you know that Doctor?' William sat down opposite him, 'You haven't seen the lass since she became with child.'

'Look son, I'd like you to leave now.'

William leaned across the table and lifted the bread knife from the side of the man's breakfast plate and turned it in his hand. 'I could tell the Master that you did not heed his instruction to visit my sister yesterday. He wouldn't like that, not with his son being the father. Or I could take this knife and cut your lying tongue out of your drunken mouth. Which is it to be Doctor?'

The doctor pushed his chair back. 'William, I'll come now, just let me get my coat.'

'You're still in your pajamas. No, you are going nowhere near her, or her child, whilst you are inebriated. But if you ever forget about the Petersons again Doctor I will not be responsible for my actions.' He leaned in once more and placed the knife exactly where he'd lifted it from before standing and turning on his heels.

16

CHAPTER THREE
Thursday 31st December

Martha was stirring a large black pan at the side of their small stove. 'I'd no idea they'd be staying on at the Big House till the after the New Year. Cook will be run off her feet. It will be costing the Master a pretty penny too.'

'Aye, but Cook has a team of staff running round her and a stove to cook on that would service Her Majesty's battle fleet. And I don't think the Master will be complaining anytime soon about money, do you? Those coal mines bring in a pretty penny.'

Their working day was nearing its end and the Petersons were preparing a large pot of pheasant soup for their Hogmanay guests: John, head gardener and his wife Annie, the Meldrums from the North Gatehouse and of course William and Christine.

Tradition would have it that they, and the coal miners who lived near enough, would first have to congregate at the door of the Big House where the Master would dispense a pail of coal to each household, a dram to each male worker and a gin to the women folk. But on this Hogmanay it was snowing heavily and over six inches of the stuff covered the paths to the Big House.

'Are we taking the bairn?'

17

'Of course we are taking the bairn Robert. And why wouldn't we, can you tell me?'

'Martha, you know fine well what I think. Do we want to show off the Master's son's offspring to all and sundry? What do you think the Master will make of that?'

'Would you rather we hid the bairn in the trees?'

'I'd rather this whole affair had never happened and I want to see an end to it.'

'Husband, when are you going to get it through that head of your that Thomas and Mary are in love. Have you not seen that young man's face when he sees her?'

'Don't be stupid Martha, what sort of a future do you think that young man has now? He'll be away from here before the Spring is upon us. And as for our daughter, what of her then?'

'Did you know that William and Christine want to take the wee one to Leith?'

'William mentioned that.'

'And what did you say?'

'Maybe it's for the best.'

'Maybe it is and maybe it's not. I wonder what Mary thinks about it? Nobody has thought to ask her, the child's mother.'

'She's only eighteen and a bairn herself. You can't expect her to make decisions like that.'

'Decisions that will affect her for the rest of her life?'

As Robert was about to answer there was a loud knock on the door and William and Christine stepped in, both covered in snow.

'Not working tonight father? It's a wee change not to hear that infernal noise from your loom.'

'And a Happy New Year to you too son,' answered Robert. 'Or it soon will be once we've got the Master's hand-out over.'

'Is that pheasant that I'm smelling mother?'

'Fine well you know it is. Where did you find the pheasant son?'

'At the wall of the estate. The dogs must have missed that one but it obviously had enough breath in it to lowp that wall and it must be all of ten feet high.'

His mother gave him a look of doubt. 'It's a wonder you didn't get shot. There's enough guns on the estate just now to arm a battalion of Fusiliers.'

William ignored the warning. 'Is that your own bread I'm smelling from the oven?'

Like her mother before her and her mother's mother, Martha made her bread in an old biscuit tin. 'Fine well you know it is, but keep your paws off till we're back from the hand-out. I've done a black bun too.'

'You're very quiet tonight Christine,' said Robert.

'I'm not much for Hogmanay Mr Peterson.'

'Well, we'd had better get going to the Big House or those miners will drink their fill and ours if we're not there.'

'They deserve to,' whispered Martha, leaning down to pick up young Thomas from his cradle. She held him tightly before pressing him to Mary's chest then removed her shawl and wrapped it around them both. 'Can't have you and the wee one catching cold now, can we.'

'But what about you Ma?'

#

Robert was the last out of the cottage. As he closed the door he looked to his family as they trudged through the snow towards the Big House that lay at the far side of the forest. He didn't want to go to the Master's yearly handout, particularly when the man's Edinburgh guests would be duty bound to enjoy the spectacle. He wished he could have talked Martha from having the child with them too but she could be a stubborn one when it suited and he knew it was pointless to object further - having Thomas there was obviously something she felt very strongly about.

19

He felt for Christine too. She obviously couldn't have children of her own and she and William could give Thomas a life that he wouldn't get on the estate with Mary. And he was getting old and couldn't keep at the loom for much longer, and when that day came it was anyone's guess what would happen to them all.

He'd heard of the new wire-weaving in Leith. The steam ships that filled the docks were in need of the new wire ropes and that brought with it tales of work and good pay. Not that Robert would ever see it. Sixty-three years of age and almost done.

It took the family almost half an hour to reach the Big House. As predicted the Havington family, their servants and their guests stood under the portico, sheltered from the snow. The servants stood in front holding trays, some with whisky and some with gin. From the sound of the miners it seemed that many had had a few prior to their arrival. Buckets of snow-topped coal lined the full length of the house; the number of buckets representing the number of families present.

Mary tried to see behind the servants for a sign of Thomas but as yet could not see him. 'There's no point in looking daughter, Thomas will have been well warned not to be here tonight,' whispered her mother.

As the servants walked down the steps towards the waiting workers, the workers moved forward as one. The first servant held out his tray but before any one of the workers could reach it the tray was removed from the servants hands. Thomas Havington had come from around the side of the building and now held the silver tray. He walked straight to John the head gardener. 'Take this home John. A servant will bring your coal in a wee while.'

The young man then walked along the row of freezing workers until he reached the Petersons. Stopping by Mary he took a small pouch from his jacket and tucked it into her shawl. He didn't speak. Robert was about to object when he felt Martha's elbow in his side.

Thomas turned, walked up the steps of the Big House and squeezed through the throng of ladies and gentlemen.

\#

Thomas Havington left the Big House the next morning and walked alone in the snow to St. Davids Harbour where he paid the only skipper there to take him across the few miles of the Firth of Forth to Leith. His old Edinburgh Academy chum Iain Cockburn would see to look after him until he could find his way.

CHAPTER FOUR
Thursday 25th March 1869

No word came from Thomas Havington yet the snows had melted and the snowdrops and aconites spread their hope across the forest floor.

If any of the servants in the Big House knew of his whereabouts they were not saying and the Petersons had seen neither hide nor hair of the Havington family. Robert no longer delivered his damask personally but instead handed them over to the Mistress's manservant at the cottage door.

His work was getting harder too. John the head gardener had died in February, killed by a falling birch that could no longer take the winds that howled in from the Forth. Both John and Robert knew that birch was long past its best but it had been John's father who had planted it and he could not find his way to cut it down.

Robert, as assistant forester, as well as damask weaver, would have to see to the woodcutting. The Master had not employed another gardener and would not until the growing season. But that season was now upon them and a head gardener would be starting. The Master had a reputation for the finest gardens in Fife and reputation was everything. Even if that meant that Annie, John's widow, would have to leave the gardener's cottage.

Martha Peterson had offered her a corner of her own house but Annie was adamant she would be fine in Dunfermline amongst the weavers. She'd been offered room and board in a weaver's cottage next to where the Carnegies had lived prior to their emigrating to America. Her keep would be paid for by cleaning and cooking and anything else the weaver, who'd not long lost his wife, could think up.

Robert knew the man and he was not well liked. One of the few weavers to refuse Free School attendance he'd scoff at the men who'd bothered with reading and writing.

They'd not seen Annie for over a week and when she knocked on their door to say her farewells, neither Martha not Robert moved to answer her knock. 'You'll have to answer the door woman!

'Only if you will turn that infernal machine off.'

'Annie it's you, come away in. My husband is just finishing at the loom. I've some things for you to take with you. I've a jar of vegetable broth and some bread and cheese. Robert has been down to the harbour for some herring.'

'If you don't mind Martha I'll be getting on my way. It will take me the best part of the afternoon to get to Dunfermline.'

'Just a moment.' Martha disappeared into the cottage. When she returned she handed her friend a few coins and a bottle of herbal medicine. 'Please take it Annie. It's not much. I've got a wee jar of my medicine for you.'

'You didn't have to do that.' Annie turned and began walking away before turning back. 'How is Mary getting on in the Big House?'

'It's too early to say, she only started on Monday assisting Cook, among other things.'

'A lot more other things no doubt. Has she heard from Thomas?'

'Not one word and she dare not lift his name up there in the Big House. She says he is never mentioned.'

'And young Thomas, how is he?'

Martha could not bring herself to discuss the bairn. I'm sorry Annie but I must finish threading those bobbins for Robert. I'll wish you a good day and a safe journey.'

Annie saw the pain in her friends face and turned towards the large ornate gates of the estate while Martha leaned on the doorframe of the cottage and watched her turn westward onto the road.

\#

Mary had just finished laying out the afternoon tea in the drawing room when the Master's voice sounded behind her.

'Mary, have you heard from my son?'

'No My Lord.'

'Not a word?'

'No My Lord.'

'How are your father and mother?'

'Father is working at your damask and mother is looking after Thomas.'

Mary could see that the Master was struggling to pull himself away from her and watched intently as he looked around the large circular drawing room before he spoke again.

'And how is the baby?'

'Thomas?'

'Yes.'

'He will be going to Leith to be with William and his wife when I have stopped the feeding.'

CHAPTER FIVE
Thursday 12th August

Thomas and his old school chum Iain Cockburn had left from Leith on the SS Morna bound for Wapping, London on the 20th of January 1869. The waters of the Firth of Forth were calm that day but when they reached the North Sea, a turbulence arose which forced Thomas to spend much of the journey in their first-class cabin.

Iain on the other hand seemed unconcerned by the swell and spent the day on deck with the soldiers from the Royal Scots whom they'd seen on Victoria Quay prior to boarding. When Iain did return to the cabin he'd obviously been drinking and fell to his bed without a word.

He'd previously told Thomas that their sponsor Sir Algernon Hyde was awaiting their presence in Wapping. It was Sir Algernon who had acquired work in the London Stock Exchange for Iain and it was Iain who assured Thomas that it would be no time at all before he too was an employee of that famed institution.

On their arrival at Wapping, Thomas woke his chum, much to his chagrin, and they disembarked to meet their sponsor. As it was, Algernon was nowhere to be seen, but a porter arrived and asked if he could take their luggage and informed them that he was to escort them to their temporary accommodation.

That accommodation turned out to be a small room on the first floor of a busy tavern, which seemed to please Iain no end as he announced that the hair of the dog that bit him was just what he needed.

The porter had informed them on their way to the place that their accommodation was somewhat down at heel but that it would be very temporary. As it was, that turned out to be the case and within one week of arriving they were ensconced in a lovely Georgian terraced house within two hundred yards of Capel Court and the Stock Exchange. They had the privilege of having the house to themselves and for that privilege they were asked to pay a mere twenty pounds per year.

Thomas's companion turned out to be correct about his pending employment with the Stock Exchange and within a few days of Iain beginning work, he too was dutifully employed.

He was not however on the same trading floor as Iain who was engaged in trading with America and the Colonies whilst Thomas was on the ground floor, designated trading in rail and industrial stock in the home islands.

The recent invention of the electric telegraph made Iain's trading with distant continents so much easier and quicker than it would otherwise have been only a few years before. He explained to Thomas one evening, when he was somewhat inebriated, that much of his work was trading between the East India Company and foreign markets. When Thomas told him he'd read much on the opium trade between India and China and asked if Iain's work included the opium trade, his friend changed the subject and discussed in its stead the coming meeting with their sponsor.

#

Thomas's expectations of his new life in London were not quite what actually transpired, and if he were openly honest he would also admit that he was missing Mary, but in the company he found himself, that would be a step too far.

For some reason that he could not quite put his finger on, he felt he could no longer rely on his companion to share his innermost thoughts and had learned that Iain had very different ideas on many things and in particular how life should be lived which in Iain's words was "to the full".

In truth, Thomas had never felt so alone and longed for home, but his dramatic departure from Fordom would never allow for that and he began to believe that his only escape from the confines of his new life, a life spent alone in an empty house, in a busy city was, as his father had suggested on their parting, to write home and to always keep a journal. Consequently he'd bought himself one, which he'd not looked at, until now.

Journal 12th August 1869

I have thought much on my father's final words as we parted, "Please write Thomas," and they echo with me always. But my father is a writer and I am not, well not until today.

Iain has gone to the country estate of Lord Longfield at Stenborough Hall for the Glorious Twelfth and I find myself truly alone for the first time since leaving home. So I have decided to document what has been happening to me since my arrival in London.

I have not yet met with Iain's friend Algernon Hyde, other than a brief glimpse at the hall, but he does seem to be exerting more and more authority over us, though Iain doesn't believe so. Last month he told me that Algernon had invited us to a meeting of "like-minded souls", or that was how he'd put it. The meeting was in a private room in the Freemason's Hall in the city. Once there we were introduced to a number of men who seemed to know much about us.

After a rather lavish supper the servants appeared again and removed the large dining-table from the centre of the hall and placed chairs in rows facing the entrance. Then one of the gentlemen present guided us both to the front row and beckoned us to sit.

We waited for some time before the door opened and in came an elderly, somewhat rotund, gentleman of the cloth. This was my first sighting of the Reverend Henry Solly. He took his place behind a large desk, sat down and looked thoughtfully around the gathering. It must have been a full minute before he stood. He then went on to describe how to deal with the Unemployed Poor of London, and with its rough and Criminal Classes.

The Reverend Solly described in detail his wishes that his Charities Society differentiated between the deserving poor, as he put it, and the undeserving poor. Part way through his lecture I stood to present a point but he asked that I wait until the end of his lecture; which I duly did.

As the Reverend reached the end of his lecture I stood again, despite Iain taking hold of my jacket to prevent me. I explained to Reverend Solly that I found it despicable that a man of the cloth should dare discriminate between the deserving poor and the undeserving poor. Was it not for God himself to decide who deserves the benefits of our labour? Not surely a mere man of God?

Iain continued to try to pull me back into my seat as conversations and objections arose from the crowd of gentlemen behind me. It soon became obvious to me that most there were in agreement with Reverend Solly's argument and I sat down.

However, the Reverend Solly suggested that I did not hide my light under a bushel and asked me to stand up. Apparently he was very interested to hear what I had to say on the matter. Then he asked me to leave my contact details on his table and invited me to come to their next meeting to enable him to enlighten me further. But I remained seated and remained silent in the hope that his attention would be drawn elsewhere.

That was when I heard Mr Hyde's voice for the first time. 'From this young man's accent he obviously doesn't come from these parts and must be forgiven for not understanding the full extent of our problems here in London.' The voice had come from the rear of the gathering.

The Reverend asked him who he might be and he replied immediately. My name is Hyde, Sir Algernon Hyde.

By the time I stood and turned to see our sponsor he was leaving the room and I merely saw the back of his beige overcoat and black bowler hat.

Now more than six months have passed and I have still not met Algernon Hyde and now see less and less of my companion Iain as he seems to find his pleasures in the many taverns and gentlemen's clubs dotted around Capel Court.

CHAPTER SIX
Wednesday 1st September

'Good afternoon William and a happy birthday.'

'Thank you mother.'

'You are all of thirty-four years old son.'

'I am that.'

The noise of the loom stopped suddenly.

'That's better, I can hear you properly now mother.'

Robert walked from the loom and handed William a book. He turned it this way and that in his hand. 'Queen Victoria's tour of Scotland 1842'

'I bought it from a passing bookseller only the other day. He always knocks our door on the passing between Kirkcaldy and Dunfermline. It's as well he rides a strong Clydesdale; those books must weigh a ton. Anyway I've lightened his load slightly.'

'Your father is never done buying books William,' added Martha. 'We've more books in here than foodstuffs. Isn't that right Robert.'

'You'll find a whole world in those books woman and knowledge one can feast upon.'

'Is that why you bought this book, am I meant to eat it?'

'Devour it son would be my advice.'

'I'd no idea you were such a follower of Royalty.'

'I am not. but knowing your birthday was coming up I thought you might like it.'

'Thank you for the kind thought but I am as much of a follower of Royalty as you. Maybe Christine will like it, she has a liking for the aristocracy.'

'Does it not remind you of anything?' asked Martha.

'No, why should it?'

'What about your 6th birthday when Andrew Carnegie's Uncle George took you and Andrew to see the Queen arriving at Granton Pier?'

'Oh that. Aye I do remember.'

'It was a Thursday but George Lauder had spoken with your head teacher at the Free School and you both had the day off. You turned six that day, Andrew's birthday was not until the November.'

'He's in America now, I wonder how he's doing?'

'By all accounts he is doing very well, but that is according to Cook and you know she can tell a tale or two when the mood takes her.'

'Aye, she can that.'

'Where is Christine?' asked Martha. 'I've made a nice pot of broth and the bran bread she likes.'

'She is not feeling so well mother, but she sends you her best wishes.'

'Is she nervous about leaving here for Leith? She is a Dunfermline girl through and through.'

'Maybe that and you know, the other thing.'

'The bairn?'

'Aye.'

'She is desperate for a child William.'

31

I know mother, it's all she talks about and she continually asks when I think Mary will no longer be feeding the baby.'

Robert walked back to his loom, picked up a bobbin and studied it. 'Poor woman. When is it you are moving to Leith son?'

'Next month, but Mary could go on feeding her child for another year or more.'

'Well you'll just have to collect wee Thomas when the time is right, he should be walking by then and it would save you a fare.'

'Can we change the subject husband please!' It was not a question.

'Are you getting on any better with the new head gardener father?'

'I think we've just said enough about that too.'

'Is it no better?'

'Young John Cant has brought his learning with him from the Botanical Gardens in Edinburgh and he knows how to show it off to the Mistress.'

'What about the wood cutting?'

'Oh aye, I'm still allowed to cut the wood but he has told me that if he sees you helping me he will report it to the Master as you are not employed by the estate.'

'What about you mother, are you still growing your herbs and your rhubarb in the walled garden?'

'No, that has stopped for the season now.'

'And because John Cant doesn't allow it?'

'He thinks your mother is a witch,' laughed Robert. 'Just as well we're not burning them at the stake as we used to here.'

'William, you take a seat by the fire and I'll put out your soup.'

'Please mother, if you don't mind I'll be getting back to Christine and see she is okay. Will the soup keep until tomorrow?'

'In this draughty place? Oh aye.'

'I'll make sure we are both here then, even if I have to carry her. Now I just need a wee word with the head gardener before getting back up the road.'

The door was opened and closed before either Robert or Martha could say another word to their son.

CHAPTER SEVEN
Thursday 2nd September

Journal 2nd September

I have just spent the most enlightened evening in the company of the Reverend Solly and his companions, Mister Alsager Hay Hill, Octavia Hill and Helen Bosanquet.

Never could I have imagined such wonderful company, particularly after Reverend Solly's talk on the conditions of the London poor.

I mistakenly believed that his use of that terrible phrase "the undeserving poor" meant that he wished to see those unfortunate people thrown to the wind, discarded like so much waste into the Thames. But my reading of his words could not have been further from the truth.

No, the Charities Organisation Society that he and the others there this evening represent are the antithesis of my original hypothesis.

Their concern is in how to give those poor people hope, how to help them gain meaningful employment and purpose. They are all extremely radical in their thinking and are willing to take the

Government to task to enforce positive change in their circumstance.

I was so impressed by those socially and politically aware people that I asked if I could join them and was welcomed in like a brother.

My biggest surprise came when Octavia announced that Lord Longfield was part of the group and a driving force behind many of their ideas.

Knowing Iain had been staying at Lord Longfield's recently instantly led me to believe that he too is involved in some way with the society. As it is only just after ten o'clock and he is normally not home till after midnight I will have to await the morning before I can engage with him on this exciting endeavour.

Journal 3rd September

I was so terribly excited this morning but managed to hold my enthusiasm until Iain and I were in the coffee house by the Exchange.

My companion was not at his best but that was more than often a normal occurrence, which I put down to his late nights and the copious amounts of wine that he consumed. I had hoped the news of my joining the society would pull him from his doldrums.

But that was not to be. We were seated at a small table by the window overlooking the Exchange and the coffee, as well as a brandy for Iain, had just arrived when I happily announced my news of joining the society. He did not reply immediately but went very flushed. I asked him if he was all right as I was concerned for his welfare but he did not reply.

When he did it was to chastise me loudly.

I attempted to defend myself by telling him that I believed him to be a member as he had spent time with Lord Longfield.

He took a large quaff of his brandy before continuing with his verbal abuse and repeated that what he chose to do was absolutely nothing to do with me. At this point he began addressing me by my surname, something he had not done since our school days.

I returned his attack by asking why our sponsor had invited us to the meeting with Reverend Solly if we were not indeed to be involved with the society.

What he said then, shocked me to the core. He announced that he and Algernon were at the meeting to learn from the mouth of their antithesis how not to go about saving the undeserving poor. Then worse, he said that Algernon has his own methods for helping those unfortunates, as he put it, and that he wanted to hear no more about it. Then he stood, quaffed the last drop of his brandy and left without touching his coffee.

After today I once more feel so terribly alone and wish I'd never left Fordom.

CHAPTER EIGHT
Sunday 12th September

'Why are we getting ready for church so early father?'

'Because Mary, we are not going to Dalgety Bay Kirk this day.'

'Where are we going?'

'We are going to Dunfermline Methodist Church. I was speaking with the Minister only yesterday and he would like to see us.'

'Why?'

'As you are aware daughter, I have spoken with our Minister here at Fordom about a Christening but he says that will not be possible in his Kirk because you had the child out of wedlock. Though he did leave me wondering if it was more to do with your mother's surname.'

'What are you on about man?' shouted Martha from the loom.

'Of course you don't know the legend, do you Mary? Your mother's ancestor, Isobel Kellock, was put to death for witchcraft here in Dalgety Bay in 1650. And that was very close to the spot the kirk stands now. Isn't that right Martha Kellock?'

'You don't half talk some nonsense Robert Peterson. That woman was no relation of mine!'

'You are a Kelloch, aren't you? They are few and far between in these parts.'

'You do enjoy working with herbs and potions mother,' added Mary, winking at her father.

'I'll not hear one more word out of you two. You could get me into trouble with the Master, and the Kirk.'

'You're all right wife, they don't burn witches anymore in Dalgety Bay.' Robert turned to Mary. No, the reason we are going to Dunfermline is that I saw Reverend Jimmy Walsh pass the gate yesterday and I approached him on the subject of Christening.'

'And what did this Reverend say father?'

'He said hello Robert, I haven't set eyes on you since I gave up the weaving, and that was not yesterday. Then he said he would be delighted to christen wee Thomas, but first we'd be required to attend his church, if only the once.'

'Do you know him well?'

'Aye, he knows him well, don't you Robert.' Martha had been cleaning the loom and stood up. 'I'd better be getting myself cleaned up if we're to walk to Dunfermline.'

'You'll be fine as you are Martha, the Methodists don't mind a wee bit of grime, if it's come by honestly.'

'Talking about honesty, would you care to tell your daughter how you come to know Jimmy Walsh while you are waiting for me to get ready?'

'I think that might be a story for another day, don't you.'

'Aye maybe, we are going to his church after all.'

\#

The Petersons left their gatehouse at eight o'clock and were immediately thankful that the rain of the day before had ceased and the sun, albeit weakened by September, rose at their backs.

Mary carried young Thomas close to her chest, wrapped in a bright red wool shawl that Martha had knitted for him.

The roadway had recently been resurfaced with stone chips and had been angled from the centre to the roadsides forcing most surface water to drain into the grass. Only one month before, this journey would have meant walking through mud or pools of filthy deep water.

They were adjacent to the William Coal Pit when Martha raised the subject of Jimmy Walsh again. 'Is by the pit not an ideal moment to be telling Mary the story of you and Jimmy, Robert?'

'Martha, I wasn't being serious about your ancestors being witches.'

She stood her ground and was obviously not budging until the tale was out.

Robert began with a stammer. 'Mary, I'll ask you to remember before I tell you the tale that times were very different then and the weaving families gutter poor.'

'Poorer even than we are father?'

'Much poorer. We have food to eat and a fire to warm us.'

'Yes father.'

Martha sat down on a low wall. 'Get on with it husband, we haven't got all day.'

'So Jimmy and I took it upon ourselves to visit the William pit in the evenings.'

'After midnight,' added Martha.

'Were you working the pit for the Havington's during the night father?'

'They were working the pit Mary, but not for the Havingtons. They were stealing their coal. He and Jimmy Walsh had made a wooden barrow, not much smaller than the Fordom wagons, and would come to the pit after dark and fill their barrow with coal and take it around the weavers' cottages. Isn't that right Robert. And your father would also have a book or two to hand out while Jimmy tried to convince the weavers to worship God. He'd always had a leaning for the church, even then.'

'But if the Master had found you father you would have lost your work and your house.'

'I didn't work for the Master then. We moved here from Dunfermline when William was twelve.' He turned to Martha. 'Are we going to have Thomas christened or are you for sitting there all day wife?'

\#

The family walked on through Crossgates and Halbeath to Dunfermline, reaching Jimmy's church as the congregation were entering for the service. They were seated no more than a few minutes when Jimmy stepped into the pulpit. It became immediately apparent that his previous "leanings towards God" had turned into full blown belief.

Relief only came part way through his sermon, when they learned that his message was not made from fire and brimstone but was simply a loud cry to worship from a man who truly believed in the power of God and the power of prayer to ease one's burden.

That and free coal thought Mary as Jimmy came from behind the pulpit and continued his message by pointing directly at individuals in the congregation.

When the service was over and all but the Petersons had departed, Jimmy came to the pews and sat down beside them. They waited for him to question Mary but he ignored her and leaned over to the baby, pulled the shawl from his face and stared for some moments before turning to his mother. 'Is this the wee man, Thomas isn't it?'

'Aye.'

'And you wish him christened here in my church?'

'She does Jimmy,' said Robert.

'I think Mary can speak for herself, can't you Mary?'

The young woman took an instant liking for the man. She lowered her head coyly. 'I would Minister.'

'Would Sunday next suit?'

Mary turned to look at Robert before answering. 'Yes Minister, that would be perfect.'

'Then next Sunday it shall be.' He stood to say his farewells. 'And how are you Martha?'

'I am well Jimmy thank you.'

'Have you told your lovely Mary how it is that Robert and I know each other?'

Martha's face reddened.

Jimmy turned and shook Robert's hand. He's a fine man your father, Mary, one of God's special creations. He'd have made a braw Minister and a well read one to boot. Half the folk around here might still be living in the dark if it wasn't for that man sitting with you.'

\#

When the Petersons left Jimmy's church it was going on for one o'clock. Mary assumed that they'd be turning for home and turned in that direction.

'And where might you be going daughter?' asked Robert.

'Home father, the wee one is getting hungry.'

'Mother and I were thinking we might make a day of it whilst we're in the town.'

'But what about the bairn?'

'You've not to worry so Mary,' answered Martha, 'you'll be able to feed Thomas when we get to our next visit.'

'Where are we going?'

'Father and I thought it would be nice to see Annie as we are so near. If we're not over late we might get a bite to eat too.'

It did not take them long to walk from the church to Annie's cottage but by the time they arrived young Thomas was crying the place down. 'Mother, I'll need to see to the bairn's feed.'

41

'We'll only be another moment,' answered Martha as her husband knocked loudly on the door and waited. 'I was sure Annie would be in.'

When no answer was forthcoming Robert turned, only to see Annie walking towards them carrying an open basket on her arm. As she got closer he could see that the basket was full of kale and potatoes. He could also see that the woman's face was badly bruised. He walked towards her. 'Annie, have you had a fall? Let me take that weight from you.' He stretched his arm but she recoiled.

'He wouldn't like it.'

'Who wouldn't like it?'

'The weaver. I've not to mix with strangers.'

'We are not strangers Annie, it's us, Robert and Martha. Mary has brought Thomas to see you; he's getting on for nearly a year now.'

Annie smiled but tried to hide her face from them.

'Annie, where did you get the kale?' asked Mary.

She pointed to the cottage. 'At his cousin's farm.'

'And where is that, you look exhausted.'

'Rosyth.'

'Rosyth!' exclaimed Robert, that's miles from here.' He walked back to the door and slammed his fist against it but no answer came.

'Please don't Robert, please. It will make it all the worse for me.'

Martha looked directly at her husband, a look that said enough for him to walk from the door.'

Martha stood by Annie and spoke quietly to her. As she spoke Annie's face began to brighten and her demeanour changed. She put down her heavy load, walked up to Mary and pulled the shawl aside. 'He is so beautiful Mary, just like his father and mother.' Then she bent once more, lifted the basket and moved towards the door of the cottage and whatever her landlord David Lamont had in store for her. 'David it's me Annie.'

\#

On a small wall by the side of Dunfermline Abbey Mary sat breast feeding her child. Martha and Robert kept guard at a short distance and hoped if someone did appear that it wouldn't be the Minister.

Thomas quietened almost immediately and once he'd been fed Mary's parents joined her on the wall. 'I've a wee bit bread and cheese in my bag here,' said Martha, removing a small sackcloth and unfolding it. 'It's not much but it will do.'

'As they nibbled on the morsel they watched a young man, much the same age as their son William, walk around the abbey. He had a measuring stick in his hand and was holding it up and looked as if he was trying the gauge the scale of the building. When he stopped his measuring he turned and saw them. 'Excuse me, I'm attempting to work out the strain on the foundations that a building of this size would exert. I hope I'm not disturbing you?'

'Not at all young man, you carry on,' said Robert, 'we wouldn't want to stand in the way of progress.'

'Do I know you?' asked the stranger.

'I shouldn't think so.'

'Are you not Robert Peterson, William's father? I was at the Free School with William.'

'I am that, and this is my wife Martha and my daughter Mary. The wee one in the shawl is Thomas, her bairn. And who might you be?'

'George Lauder Junior. You may know of my father?'

'We certainly do, don't we Martha. Does he still have the general store in the town?'

'He does.'

'He's a good man your father, stands up for the rights of democracy and equality.'

'Yes that's him, George Lauder Senior. He's a hard act to follow I'm afraid. I decided to break from family political tradition and went to university in Glasgow to study engineering. I'll be going to join my cousin Andrew in America soon. He says he needs my engineering skills in his business.'

'That's very good George,' interrupted Martha but we must be going now, it's a long way back to Fordom from Dunfermline.'

'Not in a coach,' answered George. 'My father's stable is at the top of the hill and he won't mind me giving the parents of an old friend a hurl home. I could be doing with the fresh air to be honest.' George turned and started to run. 'I'll only be a few minutes.'

When he returned he was sitting behind the most beautiful black stallion on the driver's seat of the horse drawn coach. 'My father sends his warmest regards. Mary, would yourself and Thomas like to ride up front with me? You'll get a lovely view of the county from here.'

Mary looked at Robert. 'On you go daughter, and mind that bairn.'

Once Mary was seated George jumped down and opened the coach door, The first thing Robert saw was a large basket on the seat. Once inside they sat down opposite the basket. 'Father said he knows of your family and Robert's work encouraging others to read. But you've not to let William near the hamper; always been a greedy one that Peterson he said.'

Martha leaned over and opened the basket. It was full to the brim with all sorts of delicacies and a bottle of French claret. Looks like we're in for a second honeymoon Martha,' said Robert.

'Not on your life Rob Peterson, not on your life.'

CHAPTER NINE
Friday 24th September

Journal 24th September

I have never had such a day on the Exchange. Everything was business as normal but just prior to lunch a steady crescendo of voices began and soon my colleagues were rushing here and there across the floor.

Still considering myself to be relatively new to trading I decided to remain behind my desk and await the results of such fuss. It didn't take long for those results to emerge and the first and most dynamic of those was when I saw my friend Iain being marched from the building by two tall men in top hats. I say friend but in truth he has not spoken with me since that dreadful morning.

I have heard nothing of our sponsor to boot and have therefore, apart from my meetings with the Society, decided to keep my own company.

I so enjoy going to the Society meetings and have found the other members to be like-minded people whose main interest is in helping the less fortunate to succeed in life. I still cannot understand why Iain could have been so upset as to chastise me for joining their company.

At the Society's meeting on Wednesday evening I mentioned Iain as the young man who had been in my company on our introductory meeting with Reverend Solly and spoke of the gentleman who had spoken up on my behalf and how he was a friend of Iain's and was our sponsor.

The group went silent as I spoke and no-one responded afterwards. I found this very disconcerting but as I am new to these parts I remain aware that it may simply be down to cultural differences.

After today's excitement on the floor I have decided to approach Iain on his return tonight and can only hope that he has not consumed too much beverage and is able to explain to me the happenings of the day. I must be careful as I still value our friendship and remain his loyal friend.

#

'Mother, something has bothered me since our visit to Annie in Dunfermline.'

Martha was stirring the large pot which hung from the stove. She stopped stirring and turned. 'And what might that be Mary?'

'She was rightfully very upset and before we left you spoke with her and were obviously intent on keeping out of earshot of father and me.'

'Annie is a woman of my age Mary and somethings cannot be shared with others.'

'But we are not others mother, we are family?'

'There is no-one knows that more than me and if I thought what was discussed with Annie was for sharing I would have.'

'Can you not tell me now?'

'No I cannot.'

Mary lifted Thomas from his crib and pulled him tight to her breast. 'I am needed in the Big House this evening after I have fed the wee one.'

'Is everything all right in the Big House Mary?' asked Martha as she returned to stirring of the tripe.

Mary didn't answer.

\#

Thomas waited until midnight for his friend and was about to turn in when the bell-push sounded loudly. He took the carpeted stairs downwards two at a time and strode across the black and white checked tiled floor quickly. When he opened the door the two men he'd seen removing Iain from the Exchange stood with Iain's limp body hanging between them. 'We believe this is yours Thomas.' They handed Iain over to him. 'You'd do well to keep this one under lock and key.'

Journal continued

It took all of my strength to carry my friend to the sitting room, where I laid him gently on the Chesterfield. He had quite obviously been drinking heavily and was not compos mentis so I made him a strong coffee, placed it on the small table beside him and took to the armchair to await his return to sobriety.

It wasn't until six o'clock in the morning that he came round and drank the coffee. Only then was able to tell me of his day with those gentlemen. The noise and commotion I'd seen and heard in the Exchange was caused by a drop in the American gold market and foreign shares nearly collapsed. As I was trading in home stock, particularly railways, this did not affect my end of the hall directly.

When he told me this it helped explain in part the two men at the door's American accent. What he told me next was so unbelievable that I asked him to repeat his story more than once. Those men were from the Pinkerton's Detective Agency and were employed to protect American interests in London. When the American gold standard plummeted due to misdealings in New York they were charged with investigating as to whether our

Exchange was involved. As Iain was involved in trading between the East India Company and New York he became their target.

But even worse was to come. When they left the Exchange they took my friend to an Inn nearby where they had hired a private room. In the room there was a large table and three chairs and as the shutters were tightly closed, the room was dark and dingy, lit only by two large candles. On the table stood three bottles of American whiskey.

Poor Iain was then subjected to a constant barrage of questions and a consummate amount of whiskey until he collapsed. He had no idea how long he had been in that room and he was shocked and dismayed when I told him he was brought home after midnight.

When I asked if he remembered as to whether their obvious mistake regarding any misdealing in American gold was accepted by them, he did not seem the slightest bit interested. He was more concerned with what other things he may have told his inquisitors whilst under the influence of their whiskey. The more he thought on this the more angry he became until he threw his coffee cup across the room, then burst into tears.

When I asked what those other things were that he was worried about, he did not reply for some moments and when he did it was merely to beg me never to speak of this again. He then asked if I had heard from our sponsor, to which I replied an emphatic no.

After that last question he drifted into a deep sleep from which he did not awaken until noon.

CHAPTER TEN
Monday 3rd October

William and Christine had hired a farm cart to take their belongings to Leith. It was early morning and thankfully not raining when they loaded them..

Before departing for North Queensferry and the steam ferry that would take them across the Forth they stopped by William's parents to say their farewells.

It was not yet eight but they could hear the loom's rattle as they approached the cottage. Not wishing his parents to see that they'd sold most of the furniture they'd given them when they were married, they'd left the cart outside the iron gates to the estate.

When William opened the door he could see immediately that his mother had been crying. 'Morning mother, father.'

The noise from the loom stopped. 'Morning son,' answered Robert. 'you've a fine day for your move.'

'Aye.'

'Where's Christine?'

'She's on the cart keeping an eye on our things.'

'Does she not want to come in and have some porridge before you head off?' asked Martha. 'I could keep an eye on the cart.'

'No mother, she'll be fine. The cart is outside the gates.' William answered harsher than he'd meant. 'I'm sorry mother, but you know.'

'We both know,' added Robert.

William looked as if he was about to cry. 'She can't bear to be leaving the bairn. I've been talking with her constantly but there's no settling her.'

Martha put her hand on his broad shoulder. 'As I can't bear to be losing mine. Is Christine ill son?'

'If she's not, I will be soon enough. That bairn is all she talks about.'

Martha walked over to the crib, lifted the child and went towards the door.

'Please don't mother.'

'I won't be long.'

'Martha walked the long path to the gate and saw Christine was sitting on the front of the cart and staring forward. She did not turn when Martha approached.

'Are you not coming in for a wee drop porridge Christine, it's a long way to Leith and you won't be getting there until this afternoon.'

Christine turned and saw Thomas was in her arms but said nothing.

'Would you care to hold him?'

The younger woman smiled for the first time in a long time, as far as Martha could tell. 'Can I?'

'Of course you can but you'll have to come down off that cart, we'll not be climbing up.'

Christine climbed down and stood with her arms by her sides.

'Well you'll have to put your arms out if you've to hold him. You're going to need a wee lesson or two before he comes to Leith.' Martha pushed the child forward. 'Here he is.'

Given no choice his soon to be adoptive mother took hold of him.

'It was yourself who delivered him Christine. And you delivered a healthy wee boy. Don't be frightened to give him a hug.' Martha saw the tears run down her daughter-in-law's cheeks. 'Now come away in with me and stop this nonsense. It will not be overlong before the bairn is with you and William. Mary started early at the Big House so you won't get a chance to say your farewells but we will come over to see you soon enough and we'll bring Thomas. We'll have to get him used to his new abode for when the time comes.'

CHAPTER ELEVEN
Tuesday 25th January 1870

'Some hae meat and canna eat,
And some wad eat that want it;
But we hae meat, and we can eat,
Sae let the Lord be thankit.'

A rousing applause arose as Viscount Havington dug the dagger deep into the large haggis and the odour of boiled mutton filled the room. Lord Rathmore was first on his feet. 'Weel done George. A toast to the haggis and to our great Bard, Robert Burns.'

The circular drawing room of the Big House was laid out for a Burns Supper and was full of men in differing forms of tartan attire. Some wore black evening jacket with tartan trews and tartan plaid draped over their shoulder whilst others wore full highland dress and kilt.

Their ladies had been dispatched to the first floor drawing room where they were enjoying a dinner more befitting the feminine sex.

Gentlemen from across Fife and the Lothians had been descending on the Havington's Burns Supper since early in the century and they took great pride in having the best haggis this side of the Forth brought all the way from St. Andrews. The Inverkeithing apothecary had been blending and labelling a special Havington whisky since that first occasion too.

'I must say Havington you host a good supper. Maybe not quite as good as your father before you but very passable!' It was old Dalrymple from the Donibristle Estate.

'And you should know indeed Alex. Were you not at the very first supper? That would have been 1811 I believe.' The Master's reply had the crowd in fits of laugher which served to increase their drouth and another toast to the Bard was called.

#

'Ae fond kiss and then we sever,
Ae fareweel alas forever
Deep in heart-wrung tears I'll pledge thee,
Warring sighs and groans I'll wage thee.'

'Oh Mary, that was just lovely. You were always a fine chanter, wasn't she Robert.'

'She was that Martha. And you make a fine cook of the haggis. The Big House can keep their Saint Andrews' attempt. I did enjoy my supper, though a tattie would have gone down well with my neep.'

'It wasn't your supper dearest, it was Robert Burns's supper.'

'I bet that Ayrshire lad would have had a tattie or two with his fayre.'

'I've told you more than once, the crop had failed because of the July rains and we won't be getting any tatties until the new crop in May.'

'They've potatoes up at the Big House,' said Mary. 'I was helping Cook peel them this afternoon.'

'Yon gardener from Edinburgh will have covered the Master's potato crop to protect it from the rains. And there's the big wall too,' said Robert glumly.

'Cook might have thought to give you one or two to bring home Mary,' said Martha.

'She's already been warned because of the shortages in the countryside, not to remove any food from the kitchen, especially potatoes.'

Robert lifted a book from the floor. I think it's time I recited the Bard.

'Is there for honest poverty
That hings his head an' a' that?
The coward slave, we pass him by –
We dare be poor for a' that,
For a' that an a'that.
Our toils obscure, an' a' that,
The rank is but the guinea's stamp,
The man's the gowd for a' that.'
#

'Well I must say young man that was truly wonderful. I can't remember a more lively evening at the Society. I had never heard of Robert Burns.'

Thomas had volunteered to organise a Burn's supper for the Charity Organisation and had spent a good part of January finding a butcher who would be prepared to create a haggis. The aforementioned did not, in Thomas's opinion, resemble anything like the haggis he'd had many a time at home but when he mentioned this to the Society, adding that he supposed that "beggars couldn't be choosers," he was reminded instantly by the Reverend Solly that that phrase was possibly not the most apt in the circumstances.

The evening ended well with many compliments on his singing coming Thomas's way. No-one mentioned the haggis.

The organising of the event had taken the young man's mind from happenings closer to home and he was glad of it. Iain had become more and more distant and it felt as if Thomas was sharing a property with a complete stranger. He still had not set eyes upon Algernon Hyde and presumed that he was no longer in London.

He wasn't home until nearing midnight and hadn't expected Iain to be yet home so when a voice came from the sitting room he got quite a shock.

When he entered he could not believe his eyes. Sitting by the fire was who he took to be none other than Algernon Hyde. He had a glass in his hand and was sipping from it. 'Come and join me Thomas, there's something I wish to discuss with you. Do you wish a brandy.? It is from your cabinet, or should I say mine?'

CHAPTER TWELVE
Wednesday 26th January

Journal 26th January

I have not had the strength to rise from my bed this morning and have decided not to attempt going to the Exchange.

What has been asked of me by Mr Hyde goes beyond my comprehension but I fear that I cannot disclose the content of our conversation to anyone.

Perhaps if father was here I might approach him for he would no doubt know what I am to do. I could write it down here but what I have learned is so awful that I shall not even put it in my journal for fear it should be found.

I have been told by Algernon that I must join Iain on the East India trading floor immediately and that Iain will inform me of my new duties. But now, after what I have learned of my sponsor's trading practices, I do not yet know if I can ever return to the Exchange.

\#

'I must say George, from what I can remember of last evening it was one of your best Burns' Suppers yet. Old Dalrymple could hardly climb into his coach. His driver had to push quite firmly on his derrière.'

'I'm glad you enjoyed it Hugh. The ladies seemed to have a somewhat lovely evening too from what Alice tells me this morning.'

Getting on for fifty years of age, Hugh Naismith had been in attendance at the Havington's Burns' Suppers since his late teens.

'Yes, I'm only sorry my Hannah wasn't up for the journey. It's quite a trek from Dunblane and she is not at her best.'

'What is it that's wrong with her Hugh?'

'She has the gout and it makes walking very tiring for her. It is fortunate we have a loyal servant in James. He has been with us since he was a boy.'

'Yes, you've caught a good one there. I'd give my back teeth for a servant with such loyalty.'

'Have you heard from your Thomas as yet?'

'No.'

'I was hoping I might meet that girl last night, what's her name, Mary isn't it.'

'I have given Mary some time off. Her father does not keep in good health and what with the… if you would excuse me I see Rathmore is going to his coach.'

#

Martha was winding flax onto the bobbins while Mary was stoking the fire.

Robert had begun work early on the Master's newly ordered panel, which was beginning to appear from the workings of the loom.

'That is a beautiful piece husband.'

'It is Martha. According to the Master's servant it is a gift from him for the Mistress's study.'

'That does explain the beautiful pattern. Does she grow those flowers?'

57

'With the help of the Edinburgh gardener, yes.'

Mary had stopped poking at the embers of the fire. 'Aren't you still growing herbs mother?'

'I am daughter but only in the wee bit ground behind the cottage and only when the weather allows.'

'What is that beautiful pink flower that has been growing under the willow during summer?'

'That is valerian.'

'What is it used for?'

'I'm not sure Mary. It is just such a beautiful addition to our wee plot, particularly now the gardener will not allow us access to the Big House gardens.'

'Didn't William have a word with him?'

'He did daughter but William is in Leith now and the man knows it.'

Mary asked no more about herbs but began thinking of when she might be in Inverkeithing and the apothecary.

CHAPTER THIRTEEN
Saturday 2nd April

Journal 2nd April

I feel so foolish now. My last journal entry could not have been further from the truth of my situation.

Since joining Iain on the East India trading floor he has completely turned a new leaf and we are once more the best of friends. He has taught me much of trading practices between Great Britain, India, the Far East and China. This is such a different world from trading in rail stock at home.

He has told me that our sponsor's close involvement in the Exchange comes about because he is a major dealer in commodities that travel by sea from India to China and have recently found their way to our shores too. That is why he required my services in my new role as I have experience of the home market.

It's turned out that the reason I was not seeing much of Iain was that he was helping Algernon set up a warehouse by the docks that would accommodate his imports. He says it has been extremely hard work over a period of some months and he apologised for his need to quench his thirst, as he put it, after his long toil.

I am so excited for he has promised me that after work on Monday evening we will visit the warehouse and meet with Algernon. After my tour our sponsor is going to treat us to a good meal.

I feel such a fool to have mistrusted my friends so and have worked tirelessly to make amends.

#

'Mother I have brought you the thread you needed. The lady in the shop said it was the last bobbin.'

'Thank you Mary. The wee one has been fine since you left. He's such a good boy and hardly girns, despite your father's incessant noise.'

'The noise does not belong to him mother, it belongs to that loom and that belongs to the Master, though it is the Mistress who seems to feed the demand.'

'Did you meet anyone of note in Inverkeithing?'

'I did.'

'And who would that be?'

'Archibald Trump.'

'The apothecary?'

'The very one. He is such a nice man and is asking kindly after you.'

'It is said he studied scientific botany under Duncan Napier in Edinburgh. He certainly knows his plants and herbs.'

'He said the same of you.'

'I am not studied my deary. What knowledge I have of plants I picked up from John the Gardener, Annie's husband, and the wives and mothers of Dunfermline.'

'That's not what Mr Trump says. He says that you are renowned for your knowledge about these parts, so much so that two hundred years ago you might have been in danger of being accused of witchcraft.'

'He's always had a sense of humour that one. Did you see his wife Agnes?'

'No. Should I have?'

'No, they say he keeps her under lock and key and uses her for his experiments with his herbs.'

'Don't you go putting daft ideas into that girl's head Martha!' called Robert from behind the loom. 'She's only teasing Mary, pay no attention.'

'I asked him about the valerian you grow in our patch.'

'Now why would you do that?'

'I like the flower and thought, as I was speaking to an expert, to enquire if it had any herbal properties or medical uses.'

'I didn't know you were interested in herbal medicines. You have kept that very quiet lass.'

'I do find myself becoming so. Maybe it runs in the family. Cook was telling me the other day that you are the one to consult if I wish to know more about herbs as you are an expert.'

'That cook certainly has a sense of humour too.'

'What about the medicine you gave me to put on my tooth when I was in pain?'

'Listen I think that's Thomas getting restless and needing fed.'

Mary lifted her child and put him to her breast. 'Mr Trump told me that one has to be very careful with valerian as the root has powerful properties and the tincture can act as a poison. He uses it to help people who struggle with sleep and with nervous conditions.'

'He told you that?'

'Yes.'

'Well that is very interesting. Robert, do we have a book on scientific botany?'

'We do Martha, but then you know that, you have read it cover to cover.'

CHAPTER FOURTEEN
Monday 4th April

'Tis a fine night to be going to the river Thomas but a little cold don't you think? Perhaps we can partake of a small brandy at one of the dockside taverns before we meet with our sponsor?'

Thomas had never been one for alcoholic beverage but was so elated at the prospect of seeing their new premises that he agreed.

Once in the tavern Iain found them a cosy corner near the fire. 'You make yourself comfortable and I will get them in. Just as he was about to turn towards the bar he noticed Thomas's cane, as if for the first time. 'That is a very interesting cane and quite outstanding workmanship if I may say so.'

'You may.'

'Did you purchase it here in London, I don't remember seeing it before now?'

'I was given it by the Reverend Solly at our Society's meeting last evening.'

'But why, you do not require a walking aid, surely?'

'It is not a walking aid silly boy. The Reverend said it's to protect me when I am doing the work of the Society in and around the streets of the city.'

'What, are you going to hit robbers over the head with it?'

Thomas slid the rapier from the cane. 'No, I am going to run them through with this.' He pointed it at Iain.

'But you do not know how to use it.'

'Oh yes I do. I'm a Havington remember and come from a long line of military gentlemen who served with the Scots Guards. My Uncle Peter was an officer with them and it was he who taught me the arts of war, including how to fight with a sword and with this.' Thomas turned the rapier expertly in his hand.

'Well I never Havington. Why has your father not taught you how to use arms? You told me once that he had been a soldier.'

'Yes, but my father gave up weaponry and thoughts of fighting years ago. He is a writer now.'

You never cease to amaze me Havington. Anyway I'd better get them in and you'd better put that thing away. We only have an hour before we meet with Algernon.

The hour was almost up when Thomas eventually managed to convince his friend that they'd had enough French brandy.

As it turned out the warehouse was a mere stone's throw from the tavern. It sat adjacent to the river and as Iain explained, unloading their cargo from ships into the warehouse was child's play.

Thomas could hear the water tap tapping against the pier as Iain hammered on the large wooden doors. They were opened by a warehouseman in a grey overcoat and flat cap. 'Should have worn your wool coats lads, it's bloody freezing in here. He stepped aside and beckoned them in. 'Mr Hyde is awaiting your presence through that archway.' He pointed towards the back of the warehouse.

The room through the arch was large and dark, dimly lit by four oil lamps. 'Good evening gentlemen, I trust you enjoyed your visit to the tavern.'

'But how did you know?'

'You should know by now that nothing escapes my notice Iain,' answered Algernon. 'Now to business. What you are about to see Thomas is for your and Iain's eyes only. Even the man who let you into the warehouse is not allowed in here. He has gone home now, for good, we have no more use of him.' He lifted the lid from a wooden crate. 'Iain knows what this is but come and look Thomas.'

Thomas leaned over and looked in the crate. 'What is it?'

'Would you care to enlighten your friend Iain.'

'It is opium,'

'Opium! Are we importing this for medical use? I have heard of it being used as an anesthetic.'

'In a way that is true,' answered Algernon.

'In what way?'

'The people we are treating are in great pain from living and we are helping to ease their burden, isn't that right Iain?'

'Yes Sir.'

'I had no idea that I was part of such a worthwhile endeavour. Is that why you introduced us to the Society?'

'No, not quite. The reverend Solly and his entourage are our enemies in fact.'

'I'm sorry I do not understand. Are you not concerned with the same good deeds?'

'Solly and his Society are intent on saving the wretched lives of the undeserving poor and that is why you survey the streets of our beloved city each evening. Tis to gain information to enable those undeserving mortals to gain employment and status.'

'I know. But what can be so wrong with that, that you would make an enemy of the Society?'

Algernon replaced the lid on the crate and sat down. 'What is wrong with that my boy is that those wretched creatures are polluting our glorious city. A city that Nelson and Wellington fought for and your Society is merely dragging it back to the past

64

by promoting individuals who will turn London into a cesspit and encourage more of their kind to appear from the swamps.'

Suddenly what Algernon was saying started to dawn on Thomas. 'You are giving them opium?'

'Yes, but not before it is cut with some, what shall we say, chemicals to make their journey to the afterlife less prolonged.' He began laughing. 'Am I right Iain? Is that a fair explanation of our business? Of course not all goes to such a worthwhile cause. We sell the rest in Mayfair and such like and make a very pretty penny, which you will see reflected in your pay, do you not.' He continued laughing.

Thomas turned towards Iain and stood before him. 'I cannot condone such behaviour! I will go to the authorities!'

'I shouldn't do that Thomas; your life is at risk if you do.' Iain reached inside his jacket, produced a pistol and pointed it at his friend. Thomas took a step back, the look in Iain's eyes suggested that he might actually use it.

Algernon stood from the crate and walked forward. 'Do what you must son.'

'Iain seemed reluctant to fire the weapon, causing Algernon to attempt to take it from him. The pistol was still pointing at Thomas when it discharged and all three thought he would be wounded. Thomas looked down at his chest but before the gun could fire again drew his rapier from his walking cane and ran Iain through. The hilt of the blade pressed hard against his chest and it was now he who now looked down for the wound. The pistol dropped to the floor and Iain put his bloodied his hand on Thomas's hand that was holding the hilt of the rapier. He looked his friend in the eye. 'I am so sorry Thomas.'

Algernon bent to pick up the pistol. 'What in Heaven's name have you done! Iain is my son! My son! You've killed my son.' He pointed the pistol at Thomas's chest but the younger man moved swiftly, withdrawing the rapier and thrusting it into

Algernon. It was a low blow, entering Algernon's stomach, causing him to stumble backward holding the wound. He tried to aim the pistol, discharging it as he did so, but the bullet ricocheted off the stone floor and slammed into a barrel. Thomas withdrew the blade impulsively then plunged it into his attackers heart.

He stood looking at his victims for some moments before wiping the blade with his handkerchief, an action his uncle has repeatedly instilled into him, and returned it slowly into the cane.

As he gathered his thoughts a tornado of emotions befell him. His lifelong friend had pulled a pistol and was going to kill him. He was about to die. 'My God, what have I done!'

CHAPTER FIFTEEN
Friday 14th October

The changing season came early to Fordom. Trees had lost their deep green gowns by the end of September and were adorned in their autumn colours.

Some said that frost had already been seen in the glen. Some others said they'd seen ice on the stream.

When the postman knocked on the cottage door the three Petersons looked up simultaneously from their work. Mary, being nearest, was first to the door and stepped outside to greet the visitor.

'Who was it Mary dear?'

When their daughter turned she was holding a letter. 'It was the postman.' She held the letter up. 'It has a London postmark.'

'Who can it be from? Asked her mother, intrigued. 'We do not know anyone from London.'

'It's maybe from Her Majesty,' called Robert from the loom. 'For services rendered to those and such as those.'

'We'll have enough of that Robert Peterson. Your father is becoming quite radical in his old age Mary. He'll be joining George Lauder on his soap box soon enough.'

'It's addressed to me.' Mary reached to the table for a knife and opened the envelope. She removed the letter carefully and began reading. Once she'd finished she put it back in its envelope and the envelope into her pinny pocket.

Robert was the first to give in. 'Well daughter, who is it from?'

'It's from Thomas.'

Neither parent spoke for some moments. Mary bent and lifted her bairn from his crawling on the stone floor. She untied the straps of her pinny, pulled it aside, opened her blouse and began feeding.

Her father and mother both knew that Thomas should have been on porridge and soup by this time, but also knew why he wasn't. When he had no more need of his mother's milk he would be going to Leith.

'Well are you going to tell us what has happened to Thomas's father?' asked Martha.

Mary put her child back on the floor and removed the letter from her pinny. 'He is doing fine in London and is working in the Stock Exchange. He has a lovely home near the Exchange and spends most of his evening volunteering for the Charity Organisation Society.'

'I've heard of them,' answered Robert. 'There was an article about them in the Dunfermline press. They are helping the poor of London find employment and trying to get them off a life based around charity. There are many churches and preachers involved, though not all agree with their motives and feel they are too objective and tend to treat people as a statistic.'

'Does he mention the bairn Mary?' interrupted Martha.

'He does, and says he has been sending money to a savings account to the bank in Inverkeithing. I can access those savings should the need arise, but until I find out how much is in the bank I will not know whether it is enough for me to be able to look after the wee one without having to work.'

'Mary, the bairn is going to William and Christine in Leith. We have made a promise and Christine will be expecting him soon.'

'But what about me mother, do I not need my own child?'

In his normal way Robert saw the tidal wave before it hit the shore and intervened. 'Has Thomas given a return address Mary?' Her eyes returned to the letter. 'No father. I am already late for work and must go. We can speak again about Christine on my return.'

\#

Mary was away for no more than a few minutes when Robert stopped his loom and stood. 'Martha I have something to attend to in Dunfermline. I will return before Mary is home. Will you be okay with the wee one on your own?'

'Why are you doing that Robert.'

'There is something I feel I must do, something that must be done.'

'Is it your health?'

'No, but that is what we will be telling Mary tonight. In truth I am going to see George Lauder senior at his shop in Dunfermline High Street.'

'What in Heaven's name for?'

'I am going to be asking him for the fare to London.'

'You are not going to see that young man? Please Robert, you cannot. And he has not given an address.'

'Yes he has Martha. He has given the Stock Exchange as his place of work. That is where I'll go.'

'But why? What are you going to do when you see him?'

'That is for the future to decide. We will tell Mary that I have seen a doctor in Dunfermline who has given me an appointment at Edinburgh's Royal Infirmary, where they will investigate my breathing problems. I will be in the place for two nights before returning home.'

'This is not like you to lie Robert.'

'No, and I do not wish it but I must see that young man before his son disappears in the smoke and fumes of Leith.'

CHAPTER SIXTEEN
Tuesday 18th October

Thomas heard the voice calling his name as he left the Exchange for the day. It was after six o'clock and his mind was already thinking on what might befall him once on the streets later with the Society and the poor of London.

When he looked through the crowd of traders exiting the building for the person calling his name he could not believe what he was seeing. Robert Peterson, Mary's father, was standing not ten feet from him.

At first he panicked, wondering why Mary's father would have come all this way to London if not to confront him about abandoning his daughter. His last dreadful experience with Algernon and Iain had left him very nervous and for one moment he looked to his right hand for his cane, which was of course in his house where he'd left it in readiness for the evening.

He soon realised how ridiculous he was being in that he should regard the man standing before him in that way. At that moment, the sight of a Scottish damask weaver standing amongst the throng of English gentlemen as they weaved their way from the Exchange almost brought a tear to his eye.

When Robert approached he smiled broadly, a smile Thomas knew so well from when the weaver would deliver his damask to Thomas's home.

Robert's gaze moved from Thomas to the colonnaded entrance of the Exchange then back again to Thomas. It was a gaze that told Thomas the weaver thought he was doing rather well for himself. And he was.

Since the unsolved murders of Iain and his father, the directors of the Exchange had returned Thomas to the home market floor then promoted him to manager of that floor. He had been fortunate too in having the house to himself since then, apart from when he was using it as a refuge or a school house for those unfortunate souls who trudged the streets of the city. Those souls who may have become victims of those terrible people had it not been for the protective impulse that, as he had been told many times by his uncle, belonged to the Havingtons.

Not knowing what to do next he stood, almost to attention, in front of the tall figure of Robert Peterson. But when the man held out his hand to shake Thomas's and put his other hand on his shoulder, the young man almost collapsed in grief. His past stood before him in the presence of the weaver and brought waves of nausea with it. That human touch on his shoulder made him feel as if the weaver knew everything of his life, and understood it all. It was some moments before his composure returned.

When he asked the weaver why he had come, the man's answer was not forthcoming and it would take the rest of that evening to discover his motives.

\#

Having offered to take Robert to dinner the two now sat in the window seat of Thomas's favourite eating house.

They were quiet over their meal until Thomas explained that he would be going out onto the streets that evening and the reason why, Robert insisted that it would be a great pleasure if he could accompany him. He had heard much of the Society's good works and greatly admired their interventions in helping the poor.

#

Having the weaver by his side as they talked with those unfortunate souls gave him a confidence in himself that he had never before experienced. When his visitor spoke with those unfortunates they were transfixed, much as Thomas had been outside the Exchange. That same hand that had rested on his shoulder only a few hours before now rested on each one he spoke with and everything seemed to quieten and their constant agitation was gone. It was almost as if time stood still.

It was not until their return to Thomas's home that the subject of Mary and his child was mentioned. He looked for anger in Robert's face as he explained to him why he'd had to leave Fordom, but could find none. Robert merely nodded when Thomas spoke of his family and how their status was everything to them. His fathering a child to a weaver's daughter would on no account have been tolerated.

Robert said that he knew Thomas's father well and that he was a kind and thoughtful gentleman but also knew that the pressures caused by his father's standing amongst his peers and with his father-in-law, the Earl Rathmore, were such that he could not condone the birth and said he understood his father's position. He said he did not know Thomas's step-mother Lady Masterton nearly so well and only saw her when she was in the garden, mainly in the company of John Cant the present gardener.

It was what he said next that that shocked Thomas most. Mary's son was to be taken to live in Leith with Mary's brother and his wife. Robert insisted that Mary did not want this to happen but her child had been promised to them. The weaver believed that only Thomas's return could prevent this from happening.

Thomas told him of the bank account that had been set up for Mary and that he was prepared to deposit a large enough sum to enable her to keep their son at home, but he saw immediately that the weaver found his proposition somewhat absurd, as if throwing money at the problem would be enough. Robert stood and moved to sit at the dining table. He began flicking through the pile of newspapers on the table.

That was when Thomas remembered what Mary had told him about her father's deep-seated love of reading and the work that he'd done amongst the weaving community.

As he turned over each spreadsheet he would stop every so often and read a headline. That is when the subject came up that Thomas had been trying desperately to avoid. Why Robert should have chosen that particular headline Thomas did not know.

'Iain Cockburn. Did you not have a friend of that name when you were at school? I'm sure Mary mentioned his name.' He turned the newspaper around to enable Thomas to read the headline.

'I did Sir.'

'What a coincidence. And this other name, I have seen it before. Sir Algernon Hyde was he not involved in the later development of Edinburgh's New Town.' The weaver could not have missed noticing Thomas's face redden as he read the name.

At that moment Thomas felt the urge to admit to his wicked deeds and explain that it was committed in self-defence but he could not bring himself to utter the words.

Noticing his discomfort Robert asked if he was all right, causing Thomas to pretend that it was seeing Iain's name linked to that of a murder victim that shocked him. Then Robert asked him if he had not read the article in question. Thomas soon realised that he was in the company of someone who was more than a mere weaver and he would have dearly loved to remain in his company had it not been for the subject at hand. He stood and gave his

73

excuses and retired to bed, leaving Robert browsing the newspapers.

Once in bed Thomas's head began to spin regarding that dreadful night in the warehouse and he struggled to sleep. When that sleep did eventually come it did not bring rest but nightmares.

#

The nightmares were a reenactment of the death of his friend and his father but something even more worrying, they had been caused by what he'd read in the newspaper he'd bought the previous morning on his way to the Exchange. The article that had drawn his attention had him transfixed. According to the writer some recent discoveries had been made using finger-prints and it would not be long before criminals would be brought to justice using the technique.

When he was fully awake and dressed he found the weaver in the chair by the fire. Thomas did not know whether he had used the proffered bed in the study or whether he had remained awake all evening but when he offered to escort Thomas to the Exchange, prior to taking his train, Thomas accepted gladly.

They had breakfast on the way but nothing of import was spoken of until they reached his place of work. It was then Robert asked if he had made his decision as to whether to come north or remain in London.

He would dearly have loved to reply that he was coming north with the weaver but many things prevented him from doing so. Firstly he did not know if Algernon and Iain had worked alone and whether their evil would follow him north. Secondly whether he would be apprehended by the law for what he had done and would bring shame on himself, his family and that of the weaver.

As Robert turned to walk away Thomas desperately wanted to follow him and indeed may have, had not a colleague brushed against him, announcing that they were late and that the trading floor waits for no man.

As he took the stairs to the Exchange he pondered on whether he would ever see Robert Peterson again and hoped beyond hope that he would.

CHAPTER SEVENTEEN
Thursday 20th October

Almost the second that he walked through the door of the cottage on his return from London, Mary was upon him. 'Father, why did you not tell me of your illness? I could have come with you to the Infirmary. Mother could have looked after Thomas.'

'But Mary, you are still breastfeeding and that is why I didn't ask.'

Robert's mention of her continuing to breastfeed her bairn put a stop to her tirade. 'My bairn is now with William and Christine in Leith. 'I have been so worried for you father. What have they said?'

He could see she did not want to speak more of the loss of her son. 'I have the beginning of pneumonia and that I must stop working the loom.'

What Robert had just told his daughter was no lie but he'd not had to go to Edinburgh's Royal Infirmary to discover his diagnosis. He merely had to look at the death notices of the Fife Press under the heading Hand-loom Weavers to know what was wrong. 'When did they take the bairn?'

'Yesterday. I can take more work at the Big House father and earn more money. You must stop with that loom.'

'We'll have to see. Where is your mother? I did not see her on my way in the gate. I take it she is at the Big House.'

'She's not been there since the bairn left. She has gone to Dunfermline taking medicine to Annie.'

'Is Annie ill? I wouldn't be surprised if she is the way David Lamont treats her.'

'No, Annie is well enough, when she is not being beaten. The medicine is for her employer. He's not been well for a wee while and spends much of his time in bed sleeping. Annie has been giving him herbal medicine.'

'I didn't know that.'

'Mother didn't want you worrying about Annie on top of what you are dealing with yourself.'

'Your mother is not qualified to treat the man if he is so ill. What is she giving him?'

'I don't know.'

'Well I suppose she knows well enough.'

'When you called her a witch were you making a joke father?'

'Of course I was. But it is the truth that her ancestor was burned at the stake here on the edge of the estate.'

'Could she be helping Annie by treating that horrible man?'

'Now Mary, enough of that. Your mother does not have that wickedness in her.'

'William came over yesterday. He told me all about Christine and her trouble. He said that if I wanted I could visit the bairn regularly.'

'From what you said I believed that you were going to use the money that Thomas was putting in the bank to help look after the bairn yourself. I did not know they were coming for him so soon.' Tears began rolling down his daughter's cheek. 'Oh Mary, come here.' Robert hugged his daughter until it seemed that he was not for letting go. 'We are going at the weekend to see him, you and me and mother, if she wants too.'

'She may not wish to this soon.'

'She may not want but we need to see where he is living.'

\#

Martha and Annie were standing in the small bedroom of her employer's cottage. 'He certainly doesn't look well Annie. Is he getting up at all now?'

Although it was only mid-afternoon Annie's employer was sound asleep in bed.

'Only to use the toilet out the back. I am feeding him soup and bread as you suggested and giving him his porridge with your medicine in.'

'He'll hardly have the strength to hit you while he is laid up like this deary.'

'No, but he has a fine voice for shouting when he can find the strength. He has always been very physical and does not like being stuck in bed. Do you think your medicine will help him recover?'

'Possibly. It may take a wee while though but I am sure it will, eventually.'

'What is it you are giving him?'

'I am sorry Annie but we herbalists must keep our remedies secret for fear of being copied.'

'I am not going to tell a soul Martha.'

'Neither you are. It is a mixture of valerian blended in rhubarb juice.'

'I've never heard of valerian?'

'And you the wife of a gardener.'

'I have never been interested in gardening, as you well know. How is the new gardener getting along?'

'John Cant? He's all right I suppose but he stopped Robert making extra pay by being assistant forester. The Mistress spends a lot of time in the garden since John Cant began work on the estate.'

'Why would he not want Robert…oh I see. She didn't spend much time with my John.'

'No. Your John was a lovely man Annie.'

'Aye, he was.'

'Do you remember that night at the Big House when Thomas Havington handed your John the tray of drink?'

'I do Martha. He is a lovely lad that, despite what has happened. I think he loves your Mary.'

'Perhaps. You must not breath a word of this but Robert has gone to London to see him. He should be home today and may have Thomas Havington with him.'

'Is he going to force him to come home?'

'No, of course not Annie but he is going to speak to him. What he doesn't know is that the bairn has already gone to live in Leith with William and Christine. They left yesterday.'

'Oh Martha, I am so sorry. What will Mary do now if the bairn's father doesn't come home?'

'She will keep her job at the Big House, and I must be honest Annie, without her pay we could not manage. Robert is not well.'

'He has not been well for a wee while now.'

'No. The Master wants to see him tomorrow.'

'Does he know where he is?'

'No, he thinks that Robert is at the Infirmary in Edinburgh. As does Mary – it was easier.'

'Well whatever they give him at the Infirmary, I hope it is not valerian in rhubarb juice, he may never get up again.'

Both women laughed aloud as Martha hugged her friend, lifted her woven basket and left.

CHAPTER EIGHTEEN
Friday 21st October

Robert trudged the well-worn path through the early-morning forest towards the Big House and his meeting with his employer. Frost-covered leaves of autumn crunched beneath his boots as he walked.

He stopped for a moment beside a copse of birch trees and put his hand forward to touch the moss that clung to the small branches. The tree that had killed his friend John the Gardener still lay in the grass, now covered in fungus; a fungus that would slowly devour it. Robert had never spoken the words but he sorely missed his old friend.

Under his left arm the weaver carried a roll of material, one he'd worked on throughout the night to finish. It was a gift for the Mistress from her husband. It was woven from flax that had been dyed to give a background of deep pink for the varied coloured flowers in the foreground.

Robert new that this piece of damask would be his swansong and he'd worked it so finely that even Martha had to admit it was the most beautiful cloth she had seen, but that was only after she'd complained about the infernal noise of the loom.

He walked slowly up the few steps of the portico to the doors of the house and pulled on the bell. When a servant answered he did not acknowledge the weaver but merely stepped aside to allow him entry.

A few steps from the doors Robert stopped and looked around the circular room. Paintings adorned the cream coloured walls. Most of those were portraits depicting military gentlemen in full dress uniform. The present Master was not one of those. His portrait depicted a man at peace, sitting behind a large mahogany desk. He was wearing a dark suit and red velvet cravat and was balancing a feather quill over a piece of parchment. When the real George William Havington spoke Robert almost jumped.

'Good morning Peterson. I see you are admiring my ancestors. A tough lot the Havingtons.'

'Good morning My Lord.'

'I think on this occasion we could perhaps dispense with formalities. We've known each other a long time Robert. Come to my study.'

Robert followed him across the room to a door in the far corner.

'This is where they put me for my sins. Not so much a study, more a garret.'

When they entered the room Robert saw that George William's study was bigger than their cottage. His employer walked to his desk, the same desk in the portrait, and sat down. He opened a wooden box, produced a large cigar and rotated it for a few seconds above a lit candle. 'I do prefer to toast my tobacco slowly before indulging. Do you wish one?' The Viscount did not wait for an answer. 'Do you know why I have asked you here this morning Robert?'

'Is it to do with my failing health?'

'What is wrong with your health man?'

Robert thought his employer must have developed acute deafness in his older age as one could have heard the weaver wheezing from Dunfermline. 'I am in the early stages of pneumonia.' He looked at the Master's cigar as he said this.

'I did not know that. Is it serious?'

'Yes my Lord, but I have many good years in me yet.'

'That is what I wanted to speak to you about. We have been visited by the owner of the Pilmuir Works in Dunfermline, I am sure you will have heard of it. He came with samples from their steam looms. Lady Masterton liked what she saw and in future is going to order our damask from there. It is very reasonably priced and they have a much greater variety of materials. But then Lady Masterton knows more about that than I do. Mere writers do not fuss over such things.'

Robert did not ask about the quality of the garments but walked to the desk and placed his damask piece on it.

'I wove this. I believe it is for Lady Masterson.'

His employer made no move to look at it. 'Thank you Robert, I will have one of the servants take it to her. Talking of servants, your Mary is doing a grand job. She is extremely versatile and can turn her hand to anything.' The Viscount thought for some moments. 'How is her child?'

'He is no longer with us.'

'What! Has he died?'

'No, he has gone to live in Leith with my son William. Did you not know that My Lord?''

'William, oh yes. He will make a fine father.'

'Step-father, your Lordship.'

'Mm, I wish them well. Now to the point in question. I have asked you here this morning because I am terminating your employment for the reasons I have given regarding our recent acquisitions from the Pilmuir Works. But I want to reassure you that you are in no danger of losing your home. We will of course remove the loom which should give you more space. Now, if there is nothing else, that will be all.'

81

'Yes My Lord,' answered the weaver, turning to leave.

'You have been with us for many years Peterson, have you enjoyed working on our estate?'

As he turned to answer Robert began coughing and could not stop.

'I'll tell Mary what has happened and why. Now you'd better get yourself home.'

#

When he left the Big House Robert did not walk northward to his cottage but turned right. The Glen was still in darkness as he headed down the steep side. When he got to the stream he sat down on cold stone, picked up a twig and threw it into the murky, ice-cold stream.

CHAPTER NINETEEN
Monday 24th October

Robert did not return home until evening that day, which was no surprise to Martha as she had a good idea what would befall her husband at the hands of his employer.

But for Mary it was a different story. She did not know, though rumours had abounded in the Big House, rumours about her father and what had happened to him. Yet the only concerned voice was that of Cook who, as a means of saying how sorry she was, gave Mary a large piece of venison to take home to her Pa.

Now Monday had come after a long evening of talking and planning for their future. Robert reassured them more than once that their home was secure and that they'd have, as the Master had said, more space and be without that incessant noise of the loom.

Both her parents tried but there was no consoling Mary. Martha, normally the calming influence, could not calm her daughter's anger. She hoped that Mary's duties at the Big House would keep her busy enough to take her mind from her father's health and work and what had happened to him. Had she but known what was about to happen when Mary returned to work she may not have wished for her daughter to be there at all.

First thing Monday morning Mary was just through the tradesman's entrance and had not yet met a fellow servant. Her attention was immediately drawn to a piece of material lying half in and half out of the kitchen waste bin. It was her father's damask, the piece he'd been asked to make for the Mistress.

'Are you all right dearie? You look like you've seen a ghost.' It was Cook.

'Perhaps I have Cook.'

'Why, what's happened?'

Mary bent into the bin and lifted out the damask. 'My father made this for the Mistress. He was up all night on Thursday finishing it.'

'The Mistress has just passed this way, it's a wonder you didn't see her on your way in.'

'That must have been when she dumped the damask.'

'Never mind lass, it's as well it was you who found it, you can just take it home again.'

'I can't do that Aggie, it would break my father's heart. If it has not been broken already.'

'I am so sorry what has happened to your father. He is a good man. Did he enjoy the venison?'

'Aye, we all did, thank you. Mother made broth with it too. Where was the Mistress going at this time of a morning that she could have dumped my father's work in the bin?'

'I think she was maybe heading for the walled garden and John Cant.'

'Oh, I see.'

'Aye it's the early bird that catches the worm, isn't it hen. Some say he has spelt his name wrong, that it should be John Can.'

Cook's remark brought a smile to Mary's face, but only for a moment. Folding and putting her father's work into her pinafore pocket she turned towards the corridor and her daily chores.

CHAPTER TWENTY
Thursday 15th December

I cannot believe what has just befallen me. Tonight I have been forced to leave the street and those poor wretches unattended. And tis so near to Christmas and so cold and I have promised them sustenance.

But I cannot go back there, for tonight I thought I saw the warehouseman, the one who'd been there that dreadful evening, and he was watching me.

I have felt for some time as though someone was following me but each time I turned there was no-one there. It was not until tonight, when I entered that final lane, that I saw him standing amongst a group of men and though I have seen many ruffians on the streets of Edinburgh, I have not seen any who looked as evil as those people.

I am sorry to say that I obeyed my immediate instinct and turned the other way and did not stop running until I arrived home.

What should I do? What if it was a mere apparition? My nerves have not been good of late and even the Reverend Solly commented on how tired I have become.

If truth be told I have not been the same since the visit from Mary's father. I cannot get him, nor Mary, from my mind. I see from my bank account that she has withdrawn no monies and I fear for her and for my child's health.

'Perhaps if I can get a good night's sleep all of this nonsense will vanish much as it appeared. After all, why would that warehouseman want to be in my company? He had been dismissed by Sir Algernon when he had no more need of him.'

I will write to the Reverend Solly first thing tomorrow and apologise.

Oh I do so wish that I could have gone north with the weaver.

CHAPTER TWENTY-ONE
Tuesday 1st May 1871

From the day that Mary had found her father's damask piece in the kitchen bin, she began making her plans. Winter on the estate brought short, dark days and extreme cold and that was not the time to be putting her plans to fruition. No, she thought, what I am about to do it requires a special time of year, a time of blossoms, new growth and a time for lovers.

Since John Cant had taken over as Head Gardener the landscape gardens and the walled garden had been declared out of bounds to all estate workers, unless directly supervised by him. He had brought a younger cousin from Edinburgh to assist him and had convinced the Master that he was all that was required. The Mistress gave this her full backing.

The Viscount had not taken much convincing to give Mary the day off to escort her father to the doctor in Dunfermline. She took no pleasure in lying to the Master for as it was, Robert's ailment had improved greatly since the loom had stopped and there was no need for a doctor in Dunfermline or any other Fife town.

She left the cottage at seven, her normal work time, so as not to arouse her parents' suspicion. Her mother was making the porridge when she left and her father, who'd taken to lying later in bed was sitting pressed against his pillows reading the Rights of Man.

Mary had previously reconnoitered the gardens when John Cant had taken one of his many trips to Edinburgh, and had found, from the detritus left behind in the greenhouse, the place she would have to be if she wanted to return her father's damask to its rightful owner.

She hid in a rhododendron not two yards from the greenhouse doors and smiled to herself when she saw the Mistress approach. The Lady was carrying a posy of bluebells. Though it was nearing eight the gardens remained in shade because of the high brick wall of the garden and its overhanging trees. She watched John Cant light a candle and place it on a bench which had been cleared of the pots of geraniums that Mary had seen on her last visit.

She watched the Mistress enter before counting the seconds on her fingers. Mary then moved from behind the bush and into the greenhouse. The Mistress was lying stretched out on the bench with her skirts up around her waist whilst John was standing before her with his trousers around his ankles.

'Lady Masterton, I hope you don't mind my intrusion but I have just found the damask piece my father wove for you the day he gave up weaving. I remember him weaving the whole night to be able to present this to you.' She produced the small roll of material from her pinafore. 'I'm not sure how it could have got there but I found it that morning on my way to the house and when I saw you coming here I wanted you to have it. I'm sure you must be delighted it is not lost.'

'Mary…'

'Yes My Lady.'

'John and I were just…'

'Oh, I am sorry to interrupt My Lady, I can see you are very busy. And John if you are having trouble with your belt, I'm sure my father could do a repair. Anyway, I'll not trouble you both further. My Lady if you require my services you will no longer find me in your chambers. Cook has offered to teach me to cook and I will be spending my time in the kitchen from now.

CHAPTER TWENTY-TWO
Sunday 18th August

Journal 18th August

When I read back my last journal entry, which I have done often since that night, I feel so ashamed of myself.

After writing I did not go back onto the poverty-stricken streets for some days, until the Reverend Solly visited my home and was able to convince me that I should go back.

Thank God that he did for so far I have not set eyes upon the warehouseman.

Much has happened to me at the Exchange since the new year began, I have received another promotion and am therefore able to put more savings into Mary's account, though I see that to date she has not yet withdrawn one penny.

At last I have bitten the bullet and written to my father and received a reply. I told him of my work with the poor but not where I am employed as he may have disapproved. I merely wanted to let him know that I am alive and well. I have given him my address but asked he treat it in the strictest of confidence.

I am so glad that I did for in his reply he informed me that he had been, before I was born, a Captain in the Scots Guards, though he'd made no mention of his rank when I was growing up. Apparently my Grandfather, Lieutenant General Douglas Havington was stationed with them at Wellington Barracks here in London, merely a stone's throw from where I now sit. My father suggested I report to the Adjutant to explain who I am. As my grandfather had a very distinguished career in the Guards and had fought during the Peninsular Wars and at Waterloo I will be made most welcome but only if I follow proper protocol will I gain access to the barracks. That is something I am now planning to do.

One of the strangest things that has happened since Robert Peterson's visit is that I have read the whole article in the newspaper that he had drawn my attention to on the night of his stay – the article informing of the deaths of Algernon and Iain.

Had I not been so thrown by it and read the whole piece at the time, I would have been shocked indeed. According to the article Sir Algernon and Iain's bodies were not discovered in the warehouse where they'd met their end but lying on the grass verge of a nearby graveyard.

My thoughts, when I read this, were that one or both of them remained alive when I had left and they had found their way from the warehouse but died nearby. If that was not the case then someone else must have moved their bodies.

I quickly pushed that thought from my mind as it made no sense at all.

It has been a long and tiring day today though very successful and I shall now have my glass of port before retiring.

Thomas had not quite finished his evening glass when he heard a knock on his front door. Having never had a surprise visitor to his home he rushed to answer the knock with enthusiasm.

CHAPTER TWENTY-THREE
Monday 19th August

The warehouseman had not come alone to Thomas's abode but had brought with him four strong looking companions. They all entered the house immediately Thomas opened the door. His first instinct was to reach for his cane, which he kept in an umbrella stand just inside the front door.

'I wouldn't bother with that Tom, can I call you Tom? You see these chaps are tooled up better than poor unfortunate Mr Hyde and his son.'

As if on cue the men opened their coats to reveal a variety of weapons ranging from metal clubs to pistols and knives. 'You wouldn't want to get on the wrong side of those now would you Tom?'

'What do you want with me?'

'Well first there's the small question of you murdering my colleagues. Then there is the problem of us doing you a favour by moving the bodies so that you would not be implicated in that heinous crime. I believe you owe us on that score. And last but certainly not least, I am stuck with crate loads of opium and you have access to a ready client group.'

Thomas couldn't quite grasp the situation he now found himself in. 'But Algernon said that he was finished with your services and had dismissed you permanently.'

The warehouseman laughed out loud,, causing a ripple of laughter to work its way through his men. 'Thomas, do you know why I am laughing? No, well let me enlighten you. Your friends were working for me. I see that's thrown you. Your problem young man is that you hear a Cockney accent and assume the speaker to be an uneducated imbecile, but not this time I'm afraid. The idea of having Iain trade currencies with the East India Company was mine, as was the importing and distributing of opium. Your friends found the clients and received their reward by coupling profit with their philosophy of doing away with the undeserving poor. I couldn't quite grasp that one myself but it takes all sorts. In my experience opium does that kind of work itself without need for further intervention.'

'What do you want from me Mister Warehouseman?'

The man laughed again. 'Would you listen to our future Viscount lads. You can call me Eric if you so wish Tom. Eric Phippen at your service.'

'And what might that service be Mister Phippen?'

'Well I'm glad you have asked such a pertinent question Tom. Firstly, I am offering to keep you alive. Secondly, I am offering you an opportunity to keep your child and his mother in the manner they deserve by giving you the chance to make lots of lovely money, just as your friend Iain did.'

Thomas stepped quickly towards Eric with his fists clenched, causing one of Eric's henchmen to grab his outstretched arms and pin them tightly behind his back.

'I do feel for Mary and young Thomas myself, what with them being in such a vulnerable position and so isolated in that cottage in Fife.'

'How can you possibly know that?' Thomas shouted.

'You'd better keep that voice down son or you'll be having the police knocking on your door. You wouldn't want that now would you?' He saw the young man unclench his fists. 'You can let him go Fred. Now Tom, this is what is going to happen next, if you wish to ensure the safety of your child and his mother. Firstly you will speak to your directors at the Exchange and will tell them that you are once more interested in the foreign markets and in particular the lucrative East India Company and request a move to that floor. Once that is achieved you will return to the warehouse where you will be welcomed back to the business and will organise distribution of the remains of Algernon and Iain's shipment. The captain of the vessel that brought the shipment has remained unpaid and that is not good for business and it is not very healthy for us either, as his crew will not have been paid.'

'One question. How do you know about my child?'

'How do you think I know? Through your friend Iain Cockburn of course. You trusted him with your life remember.'

CHAPTER TWENTY-FOUR
Friday 20th October

It was almost a year to the day from when Robert had visited Thomas in London and had read the names of Algernon Hyde and Iain Cockburn in that newspaper in Thomas's house. Since that day Robert had pondered on the coincidence that those were the same names of people both he and Thomas knew.

Retirement had not come easily for the man who had worked solidly from the age of twelve and had his own loom, inherited from his father, by the age of eighteen. But that loom had long given up the ghost.

They'd lived in Dunfermline then and he had remained at home with his parents until he met Martha. It wasn't until their son William was twelve that Robert found a job as damask weaver to the Havingtons. He'd been recommended to them by George Lauder Senior, who had been buying Robert's damask for his shop in Dunfermline.

For twenty-four years he had worked for the estate and had known the first Lady Masterton. Though her reputation became tarnished by some, he had held her in high regard and believed that internal politics in the family were to blame for the accusations of adultery. Young Thomas was hardly out of his Christening gown before she was forced to leave the estate with her reputation in tatters.

Thomas would no doubt have heard the rumours as he grew up and it must have affected him greatly. It may be he was glad to be sent off to board at school in Edinburgh, particularly after the

Master introduced the new Mistress to the estate. She, being an Earl's daughter, was certainly a step up for the Havingtons, thought Robert, but what about poor Thomas?

It was for that reason that Robert went to the Dunfermline Press offices this day. Having brooded long and hard on that newspaper article he made up his mind to investigate the matter further.

What he found in the archives from April 1870 confirmed everything that he'd anticipated; that the names of the deceased being the same as those persons names known to him was no coincidence. What did surprise him was that Iain was Sir Algernon's son, but for some unknown reason he had been juxtaposing his given names. Iain was actually Iain Cockburn Hyde, but he did not use this surname and replaced it with his middle name.

By the time Robert had finished in the archives he was more flummoxed than ever. But that brought with it something more immediate. It probably meant that Thomas knew more than he'd said that night in London and that explained why he had such a look of shock on seeing the article.

As Robert stepped from the Dunfermline Press Office he looked around the busy thoroughfare. 'That lad is in serious trouble,' he said aloud.

'Are you all right Sir?' asked a passerby.

The voice broke him from his pondering. 'Oh aye, fine thank you.'

#

'George, I have brought the money you gave me for my trip to London. I am sorry it has taken so long to repay you.'

'Robert, I told you at the time, it was not a loan. I heard what happened at the estate and to your job. The same thing is happening all over Fife, handlooms silent and weavers put out of their homes. I am giving a talk on that very subject tonight if you wish to come along. My son will give you a ride home afterwards.'

95

'That is something that would interest me greatly George but with no way of telling Martha she would be worried, particularly with the state of my health.'

'I'll not hear of it. I'll get my servant to ride out to your cottage and let her know. I could do with a man like you on-board Robert, but there is another reason you came to see me, isn't there?'

'George, I'm not sure…'

'Hold it there, I'm just closing for lunch. You will join me? We've got a nice beef stew on the stove and might even manage a wee Leith Claret to soak up the bread.' The second he'd said this George regretted it for he too had heard of Mary's child's emigration across the Forth to Leith

#

That evening Robert was in his element in the library in George Lauder's house above the shop. He had never seen a library like it and George had given him carte blanche to browse the collection of both rare and modern tomes.

He'd enjoyed lunch with George in his shop earlier and they had been joined by his son George Junior who regaled them with stories of engineering practices and how one day he was hoping to join his cousin Andrew in America and use his learning to help him build the best engineering works the world had ever seen.

Fortunately George junior was only passing by and did not stay throughout the whole lunch, giving Robert the opportunity to raise the subject of Thomas Havington with George senior.

After George had been told the whole sorry tale and given it much thought he gave Robert his opinion. 'You must speak to Thomas's father.'

'I have thought about that on many occasions but the Viscount can be a stubborn man and may not wish to hear from the likes of me the tale of his lost son, particularly when that son is the father of my daughter's child.'

'That's it exactly.' At this point George became indignant. 'He may be a Viscount, but you are both grandfathers of that child and it's time George William Havington faced up to that. It's not enough for him to hide behind his title. He has a responsibility to that child, to his son and to you. Will you speak to him?'

It was as if George's outburst awoke in Robert a sense of self that he had not felt in quite some time. 'I will speak to him,' he replied.

#

George junior called from the drawing room. 'We are ready for you now Mister Peterson.'

When he entered, Robert immediately recognised some of the faces present and thought he'd be joining them in the auditorium. He moved towards it but was guided by George junior to the table where his father sat.

Once Robert and young George had taken their seats George senior stood. 'Gentlemen, many of you will know the man on my left but for those who don't this is Robert Peterson, previously weaver to Viscount Masterton's Fordom estate. Like many of you here Robert is now a redundant damask weaver. If you are wondering why he is sitting here at the speaker's table it shall become apparent in due course. Firstly, let me introduce my son George Lauder Junior. George has some things he wishes to enlighten us about.' He turned to his son and beckoned him to stand.

'Good evening gentlemen. For many years I have been a student of engineering but I won't bore you with my findings.'

Once the laughter had died down he continued. 'I have also been studying life in modern factory settings, factories such as the Pilmuir Works in Dunfermline. My studies have focused not on the conditions in that factory nor on the working conditions of the men, women and children employed there but on something far more relevant. If you will bear with me, many of you will know and be proud of the fact that handloom damask weavers are highly literate. You have been responsible for producing pamphlets and papers that have changed working lives for many, not least the miners of Fife so you are well read in working conditions and how to bring about change.'

Young George took a sip from the glass of water in front of him. 'This man sitting here,' he pointed to Robert, 'is responsible for much of that learning. He has been distributing literature across our county since he was a young man. It would be fair to say that most of his meagre earnings have bought books for others to read. But we do not have him here tonight to reward him, not quite yet anyway. We have a much more important task in mind.' He sat down as his father stood up.

'What my son is referring to is his findings that the weavers of the steam looms in the Pilmuir Works are no longer as literate. There is little need for it where the owners are concerned. In fact, it may be detrimental to the owner's financial self-gain if he cannot reduce the weavers' skills in communication to mere hand labour, for if you cannot write about exploitation, you cannot change it.'

His voice was rising steadily as he spoke. 'That is why Robert Peterson is here. For we, and I mean all of us in this room, must take responsibility to guarantee that the workers, yes the ones who took your jobs, learn to read and write. Without those skills they are mere fodder for the machines that are quickly becoming their mind-forged manacles!'

Every man in the room stood, all except Robert, and applauded loudly.

'Robert, do you wish to say a few words?'

'No thank you George, I believe you and William Blake have said it all.'

CHAPTER TWENTY-FIVE
Saturday 21st October

Robert did not arrive back from George Lauder's talk until after ten o'clock. Martha and Mary had remained up and were sitting by the stove when he walked in.

'Well father, a late night for you. You must be tired from your journeying. Do you want me to heat you some soup?'

'No thank you Mary. I've had supper.'

'Oh, you've had supper indeed,' answered Martha, 'and what did you have?'

'Cold roast beef with horseradish, bread and beer.'

'I thought I caught the scent of a brewer's fayre. And what was the occasion?'

'Did George Lauder's servant not tell you?'

'He said you would be dining with George and his son tonight.'

'When I was finished at the Dunfermline Press yesterday I popped in to George's shop and he invited me to a talk that he was giving tonight in his home. His talk was on Industrial Weaving; that is where I have been and it was very interesting.'

'And you got roast beef and beer. I believe Mary and I would have found that part interesting. Anyway you are looking very tired and it's time you were abed. We can finish our interrogation in the morning.'

\#

When the morning came, Mary arose to find her father by the stove reading a book on the advent of the steam loom.

'Good morning daughter. Your mother is out the back seeing to her herbs and potions.'

'I have been asked to work today as his Lordship is having guests this evening and there is a lot to do in the kitchen.'

'I was hoping to have a word with the Master today.'

'That is a great hope indeed father but not one I would hold out much hope for. The Master is keeping himself to himself just now and only appearing when duty demands.'

So it is a forlorn hope I have?'

'Yes, I think so.' Mary thought for a moment. 'What is it you wish to speak to him about?'

Things were discussed with George yesterday that I thought the Master might be interested in.'

'What was that?'

'Och, you don't want to bother yourself with such like. It's about engineering and the profit of the new steam mills and how it may impact on the landed gentry.'

'I suppose I could have a word with the Mistress, she always has her husband's ear.'

'You would have to get her from the garden first, but it would be a great help to me if you could.'

'I will try. I know that the Master takes his after lunch walk at two-thirty every day and that might be a time to catch him.'

'You seem confident he will agree.'

'I have a good relationship with the Mistress and am sure I can arrange it.'

'You are a good one Mary, you really are.'

#

'Good afternoon Robert. Lady Masterton mentioned you'd be wanting a word. What is it I can do for you? I am having guests tonight and am somewhat busy.'

In light of his Master's declaration of busyness Robert thought best to cut to the chase. 'I have been to London my Lord and I have met your son.'

'You have what!'

'Thomas. I have spoken with Thomas.'

'Get out of my sight you, you…'

'He is in trouble.'

The Master picked up a branch from the forest floor and for one second Robert thought he was going to hit him with it, before he turned and threw it as far as it would go into the stream. A long silence befell the two men that could not be breached.

Eventually the Viscount turned to face the weaver. 'Why did you go to see him Robert?'

'Because I was worried for his and Mary's child and wanted to know what Thomas, Mary's child's father, is planning to do.'

'You have a distinct nerve for a mere weaver. Thomas is the son of a Viscount.'

'Son of a Viscount or not, you and I are grandfathers to his child. We have a duty of care to them both.'

'How did you know how to find him?'

'He sent a letter to Mary in which he mentioned his place of work. I went there and met him as he was leaving for the day.'

'And where does my son work?'

'He is in the Stock Exchange in Capel Court.

'What trouble is he in?'

'He has got himself mixed up with some bad people through no fault of his own and two of his friends have been killed.'

'What friends?'

'You'll remember his friend from school, Iain Cockburn Hyde, well he is one of them.'

'Oh, poor Iain. I knew the boy well.'

'The other is his father Sir Algernon Hyde.'

The Viscount took a step back and almost stumbled down the slope to the stream. 'I have met Algernon a time or two. What happened to them?'

'They were both murdered and I believe that prior to their deaths they got Thomas involved in whatever it was that led to their deaths.' It was Robert's turn to pick up a fallen branch. He turned it in his hand, studying it carefully. 'I am sorry to be the bearer of such news my Lord.'

'I believe you are Robert. It must have taken much courage to come to see me.'

'Mary knows nothing of this situation My Lord and I would prefer it stayed that way. I do believe your son is a fine young man with a future here at Fordom, despite what has happened between him and Mary, and I would not wish to see any harm come to him.'

'No, neither would I. He has written to me and given me his address but made no mention of any dealing that could be harmful to him. I shall go post haste to London and speak with him. Now will that be all Robert? I do have much on my mind.'

'It is My Lord.'

'Then I wish you good day.'

As the weaver climbed the bank from the stream his Master called after him. 'And thank you Robert.'

CHAPTER TWENTY-SIX
Monday 23rd October

'Father, what are you doing here?'

Thomas's father was waiting for him on the steps outside his home. It had just turned six-thirty in the evening. 'I have been here for some time thanks to the new steam trains that run between Edinburgh and London.'

'You should have written, I could have prepared for your arrival.'

'In what way my boy? Don't tell me you've not been keeping an orderly home.'

'No, not that, my home is lovely, as you will see.'

'Then what?'

'I could have prepared a meal.'

'Of course, but I thought under the circumstances I could take us to an eating establishment. We have much to catch up on my boy.'

'Father, I would so dearly have loved to join you for dinner but I have an engagement by the waterfront at eight and barely have time to change.'

'A young lady perhaps?'

'No, nothing like that. I work at the Stock Exchange during the day and have another job in the evenings.'

'How interesting. I will know who to come to regarding my stocks and shares. Your new knowledge could be very profitable for our coal mines and shipping. What is your other job?'

'Look father I am sorry but I really must go. The people I am working for will be waiting. Can we meet tomorrow morning? There is a very nice restaurant not far from here. Do you have a hotel?'

'I do. Can you get some time off from the Exchange tomorrow?'

'I could have the morning off.'

'Then why don't I collect you in a cab at nine and we can have breakfast before I head north.'

'Perfect Papa, there are some very good eating establishments near here. It is so good to see you again. I have missed you.'

'As I have missed you my boy, as I have missed you.'

CHAPTER TWENTY-SEVEN
Tuesday 24th October

His father's cab was waiting for Thomas outside his house at nine o'clock. As the young man crossed the road he thought about the morning ahead, in particular about his evening job, the knowledge of which must be kept from his father. But his father was not a stupid man; he'd led men into battle and was now a writer and by all accounts, a good one. Thomas had already decided if the subject did come up that he would be forced to tell a lie and had chosen carefully from lines of work that are carried out in the docklands. The job of accountant to a cooperage fitted the bill perfectly for his own qualifications to match and by the time he got into the cab he was more relaxed.

Unexpectedly, the subject of his evening work did not raise its head as they sat the morning out in the café. But to Thomas's surprise the subject of his son did take up much of their time together. At one point, very much to his surprise, his father referred to himself as young Thomas's grandfather, though he did insist that they keep that term between themselves.

It was only as they were parting that his father asked about Thomas's evening employment. The question came so casually about what he did and where his evening work was situated, that Thomas had no qualms in telling him he was an accountant and that this was at a warehouse by the Bell Inn on Executioners Quay.

That information seemed to satisfy his father's curiosity and after telling Thomas of his own hoped for plans for that afternoon, his father took his leave.

#

It was a fine morning for a handsome cab ride through the City of London. The sun was already behind him as he headed from Bartholomew's Lane towards Wellington Barracks.

He'd enjoyed his stay here when a much younger man and soldier but that was only before it become fairly obvious to him and to his colleagues that the military was not for him.

He was relieved when he eventually plucked up the courage to resign his commission. His action was held in no disregard by the regiment as it was common practice for officers to spend a few years in the military before resigning their commissions and returning to help run the family estate. But it was a different story when his father found out. He could not be consoled. Lieutenant General Douglas Havington was a military man through and through and would have no truck with a son who wished to be a writer.

As his cab drew up outside the barracks the two sentries guarding the gate came from their sentry boxes and looked on. Havington stepped down, put on his top hat and paid the driver before turning to face them. 'Good morning gentlemen.'

'Good afternoon Sir,' came the reply from one of the men.

Havington lifted his pocket-watch from his waistcoat pocket and studied it. 'So it is.'

'What can we do for you Sir?'

'Would you mind telling your Guard Commander that Captain Havington wishes to speak with your Commanding Officer.'

Both Guardsmen immediately stood to attention and saluted whilst simultaneously hammering the butts of their rifles on the cobbled ground. The soldier who'd wished him a good afternoon stood stock still while the other turned and disappeared into the gatehouse. Within a few seconds he reappeared followed by a Sergeant. 'Do you have an invitation Sir?' the voice boomed.

'I do not. I was stationed here at one point when I was a Captain in the regiment and as I am in London I had hoped that I could just see the old place one last time.'

'And you wish to speak with our Commanding Officer, Lieutenant Colonel Makepeace?'

'Yes.'

The Sergeant hesitated for a moment. 'I will take you to the Adjutant's Office Sir. He will make that decision. Please follow me.'

'Of course.'

The two sentries stepped aside, allowing the visitor to follow the Sergeant to the edge of the parade ground and around the perimeter towards the main building.

'They didn't have those in my day in Crimea.'

The Sergeant stopped in his tracks and turned. 'What's that Sir?'

'Your sentries' rifles. It was the good old musket for the Guards in my day.'

'Snider-Enfield. Cartridge loaded and far more accurate than the Enfield P53 that your lads would have used at Crimea Sir. Kill a Prussian, or a would be intruder at three hundred yards those weapons.'

'How interesting Sergeant.'

'All part of the job Sir. Now if we can get you to the Adjutant.'

Havington said no more until they reached the door marked Adjutant's Office with the name plaque Captain Samuel Stark below.

His guide knocked hard on the oak door and waited. 'Enter!' boomed a voice from inside.'

'We have a visitor Sir.'

The Adjutant looked up from behind his desk and growled 'Sergeant I have instructed you...'

The Adjutant was interrupted by Havington following in behind the Sergeant. He leaned around the broad shoulders of the man. 'Captain Havington, ex Scots Guards. You may have heard of my father – Lieutenant General Douglas Havington, though the Peninsular Wars and Waterloo were perhaps somewhat before your time Captain.'

For a moment it looked as if the Adjutant was about to choke on Havington's words. Lieutenant General Havington was indeed well known within the regiment, and the Adjutant was also aware that General Havington was also Viscount Masterton, and this was his son. The Sergeant looked just as shocked as he stepped aside, stood to attention and saluted. 'Sir, I am sorry if…'

'No need Sergeant. Now if I may have another word with your Adjutant.'

The Adjutant stood up and beckoned his visitor in. 'If you could have let us know you were visiting My Lord, we would have prepared a welcome befitting your standing in the regiment.'

'There would have been no need for that Captain Stark.' He shook the officers hand.

'Do you wish to speak with our Commanding Officer?'

'Is he available?'

'If you give me one moment Lord Masterton.'

The Adjutant knocked on the door marked Commanding Officer, opened the door and without entering the room waited for the Commanding Officer to look up.

'Yes Samuel?'

'Sir, we have someone wishing to visit the barracks.'

'Visit the barracks! What in Heaven's name do you think this is, the bloody Arc de Triomph? This is Wellington barracks, not a holiday destination!'

The Adjutant disappeared inside the room, leaving the door slightly ajar. Havington could not hear what was being said.

When the door opened again it was the Commanding Officer. 'Lord Masterton, welcome. Please come in.' He led him into his office. 'Take a seat.'

The visitor smiled to himself as he looked above the Colonel's head at a very familiar face. A painting of Havington's father in full dress uniform looked down from the wall. 'I confess I wasn't expecting to see my father this morning'

'We hold your father in very high regard in the regiment Sir. My Adjutant tells me that you were a Captain with us.'

'I served in the Crimea before becoming Adjutant here at the barracks.'

The officer walked to a small cabinet by the window. 'Sherry?'

'That would be very acceptable, thank you.'

'You will, I hope, do us the honour of joining us for lunch?'

'I would be delighted.

'Just one moment.' The Colonel handed him the schooner of dry sherry and left the room, returning after only a few moments. 'Lunch will be in half-an-hour. I am not sure there will be many, but there may be one or two officers at lunch from your time with us.'

The half-hour wait for lunch passed quickly in small talk of the regiment before he was escorted to the Mess by the Adjutant and shown into the Ante Room where several officers were already gathered. Havington knew, because of the numbers present, that they had been summoned, and were 'On Parade' to welcome a VIP visitor to the Mess. He noted and appreciated the honour.

After only a few moments, the Mess Sergeant entered the room, made his way to the Commanding Officer's side, and quietly informed him that Lunch was ready. 'Gentlemen, let us go in' announced the Commanding Officer.

Once around the dining table he stood behind his chair The table bore the weight of the regimental silver. The Viscount remembered that the Regimental Silver was not normally laid out for lunch – this had been done especially for him. He had forgotten how well the Military did these things. The Commanding Officer gestured to him to take the seat on his right. They both sat down. Without being instructed, the Adjutant sat on the chair on the Commanding Officer's left. The other officers all took their places, it seemed in rank order. The Majors sat closest to the Commanding Officer, and those of more junior rank sat further down the table. Once seated they were introduced to their visitor by the Commanding Officer and a toast was made to Lieutenant General Douglas Havington and his son Captain Havington.

The lunch itself had barely begun when Havington looked across the table at the officer sitting next to the Adjutant. Unlike the other well-groomed officers, this man had a dark, weather beaten face and was notably older than his colleagues. Havington assumed this must be the Quartermaster. He could also see behind his large moustache that he knew the man and from the man's eyes that the feeling was reciprocated.

From that moment lunch merely got in the way for the Viscount. His main objective, to find someone who could keep a look out for his son, was sitting at the same table and he could barely wait to speak with him.

It was almost an hour before lunch was finished and they all retired to the ante-room for coffee. The Viscount was keen to speak with the Quartermaster but was aware that as he was the VIP visitor, his duty was to work the room, and spend some time with as many of the officers that had so generously entertained him to lunch. He would have to wait before he could make his excuses and break away.

When he thought enough time had been spent in their company he thanked the Commanding Officer for lunch and for the opportunity to meet so many of the officers. He went on to say it had brought back many happy memories of his time with the Regiment. However, he understood the Commanding Officer's

110

position was a busy one, that work waits for no man and felt that he could not keep him any longer from his duties. He then explained that he may have served with his Quartermaster and, with the Commanding Officer's permission, obtained directions to the Quartermaster's department. With that brief explanation, he bid farewell and set off to find the Quartermaster.

\#

'Sir, I could not believe my eyes when I sat at the table and saw it was you.'

'I've not changed that much in old age Walker. Or should I say Quartermaster? You have done very well for yourself for a lad from Dunfermline, Quartermaster indeed; very few soldiers make Commissioned rank.'

'I have that Sir, but that is in no small way thanks to you.'

'From our time in Crimea?'

'Indeed. Remember I had been accused of putting my bayonet where it should not have gone.'

'Yes, I do remember Walker, those Russian prisoners.'

'I'd not long witnessed what they'd done to our lads and wasn't having it.'

'No Walker. You were a wee bit hot headed if memory serves me well.'

'The army was going to have me flogged Sir. They said they needed an example and they might have flogged me to death if you hadn't intervened. You told them that the prisoners were trying to escape and I got off with a warning.'

'Mm.'

'The Colonel said to give you a tour of the barracks Sir. It would be my pleasure.'

'Actually Hector, may I call you Hector?' He didn't wait for an answer. 'My train back to Edinburgh is due to leave at six o'clock but there is something you may be able to help me with.'

'What is that Sir? I owe you my life.'

'My son Thomas is here in London and I believe he may have got himself involved with a bad lot. He said he is working in the evenings for a cooperage by the Bell Inn on Executioners Quay but I am not convinced. Do you think you might keep an eye on him for me.

'Of course Sir. How will we recognise him?'

The Viscount smiled as he removed his watch, opened it and took out a small vignette of his son. This was painted for his eighteenth birthday. He handed in to the Quartermaster. My son's address is written on the back of the painting.'

'Excellent Sir.'

'You know Hector, if I had been a younger man I would have dealt with this myself.'

'And pity help the people you are up against Sir, if you had.'

'Be that as it may, I do appreciate what it is you do for me. When you are next in Dunfermline you must visit us at Fordom.'

'Thank you Sir, I will do that.'

CHAPTER TWENTY-EIGHT
Wednesday 15th November

'Well, would you look at your father Mary, I've not seen him dressed up like that since our wedding day. In fact he was not dressed so well then either. Do you think he's maybe joined the Free Masons?'

'Now we'll have no more of your shenanigans Martha Peterson, you know fine where I am going. George Lauder's handsome cab should be here any moment now.'

'Another meeting of the Lauder–Peterson education revival society. I don't know why you can't hold these meetings in daylight. Have you something to hide perhaps?'

'Actually, yes is the answer to that but it is not the main reason. Most of our members are working men, including George, and can only meet in the evenings.'

'Men, what no women. Would you listen to him now Mary, "most of our members". You are getting very highfalutin for a weaver Robert. It was not so long ago we couldn't steal you from your loom.'

The second Martha said this she regretted it. She watched as her husband turned to look at the corner in which the loom had stood.

The coachman's knock on their door was welcomed by them all.

\#

'Gentlemen, we are gathered here tonight to discuss some very serious issues which have come to light regarding our brothers and sisters working in the factories of Dunfermline.'

'Don't forget their poor children George,' came a voice from the rear.

'I know some of you here may not be worshippers but if you can bear with me, we shall begin with the Lord's prayer.'

Immediately after the prayer George Junior stood. 'Weavers, it has come to our attention that some very dubious practices are now playing out at the Pilmuir Works. More companies are joining Alfred Wain, for example May and Garvald, in building more and more steam looms and putting more and more handloom weavers out of work. But that is not the worst part. One week ago Robert here delivered some literature to the workers at the factories. He was waiting as they left the premises in the evening and handed out books by Charles Dickens and asked the folk who received them to pass them around the workforce once read.

What happened next is beyond our ken. Some of the books came to the attention of the Works Manager who promptly discovered where they had come from. That same day all the people who had received a book from Robert were called to the manager's office and asked to return them to the giver. They were told, in no uncertain terms, that if they did not return the books by the end of their working week they would be asked to leave their employment.

When one weaver, Hugh Westray, who some of you may know, objected and refused the order he was escorted from the premises and told never to return. Hugh is with us tonight. Hugh, do you wish to say a few words?'

Hugh Westray stood, book in hand, and held it up. 'Great Expectations. That's a laugh, now I've none. So where did accepting Robert's kind gift get me, you may ask – waiting for a handout is my answer. My family has barely eaten this week and all because of this wee book.'

'Maybe it was not such a good idea to hand out literature at the factories,' came a supportive voice from the men gathered.

'No,' retorted Hugh, ' that's where you are wrong. It was a very good idea for it has highlighted the lengths to which those owners will go to keep their workforce ignorant.' He held up the book again. This book has got them worried. There must be something in it they fear. Or, we have to ask ourselves, is that something in every piece of literature that has ever been written? The answer is yes. The louts who escorted me from the premises found it hilariously funny that I could read and write and that I wanted more. So as I looked up at them from the wet gutter I lay in I swore that by hook or by crook I would have them read!'

An applause arose in the company that only subsided when George Senior stood. 'Hugh, there will be a basket delivered to your cottage first thing in the morning, and if anyone else here is not able to feed their family come to my premises in the High Street. Gentlemen, please do not think that I am the most generous of men. No, we have a sponsor. Some of you will have heard the name Carnegie. The Carnegies were handloom weavers, just like yourselves, in Dunfermline and were forced through poverty to emigrate to America. Now their son Andrew has accumulated some wealth. We have been in contact by letter and more recently by telegram. In his last message he expressed his philosophy of working life and this is what he said.' He held up the message and read. "Labour, capital and ability are a three-legged stool. They are equal members of the great triple alliance which moves the industrial world".

George put the letter on the table. 'Gentlemen, our sponsor, Mister Andrew Carnegie does not want the three-legged stool that is Dunfermline weaving made to topple by the inevitable shortening of one leg of that stool, which is your labour made dull through illiteracy.'

CHAPTER TWENTY-NINE
Thursday 16th November

Journal 16th November

I do not know where to turn nor what I shall do. I am in the Exchange from nine o'clock until six and after a brief repose in a local Inn I am spending the early evening at the warehouse. The warehouseman and his thugs watch me constantly as I measure the contents of each crate and set them aside for delivery to their intended receivers.

From what the warehouseman tells me the deliveries are to the premises that I have identified through my trading contacts with the East India Company at the Exchange. It would seem that although the company is trading in India and the Far East they have many contacts in London and are able to identify a ready market for their produce here.

I am only thankful that the warehouseman has no truck with serving the contents of those crates to the unfortunates on the streets and seems only interested in profit. By the time he is done with me, usually by nine o'clock, I am able to go to the service of those people who so desperately need it.

I am never home before midnight and always hungry when I arrive. Fortunately through sheer chance I was introduced to the widow who lives in the house next door and she seems to have taken a shine to me and most evenings when I return there is a basket of food on my doorstep. Though when I approached her to give thanks she completely denied that this was of her doing. She did look at me in a very strange manner but I cannot think who else may be so kind as to supply such fayre. Perhaps I should consult Reverend Solly as the Society may have taken it upon itself to look after my welfare.

It is three weeks since my father left for home and I am missing him now more than ever. He has not written since his return and I do not know whether he did visit his old regiment and if so what the outcome was. I would like to visit them myself but time does not allow me such pleasures.

I do wish he would write.

CHAPTER THIRTY
Friday 17th November

The Sergeant knocked on the door loudly.

'Enter!'

He entered the small office, stood to attention and saluted Major Walker, the Quartermaster. 'Good morning Sir.'

'Good morning James, what news?'

'For three weeks now we have observed your charge discreetly and have, as instructed, left sustenance by his door each evening. We have as yet found nothing untoward going on and the person I set to the task of observation believes that no further action is necessary. As Will is a trusted source with much experience in those things I believe it time we called a halt to the proceedings.'

'James, do you find something distasteful in my request to look to my nephew's welfare?'

'Not at all, but Will has been there every evening and until now has only witnessed some barrow boys hanging around the warehouse in which your nephew works.'

'Take a pew James. Did this Will see what the barrow boys where doing outside the warehouse?'

'They were just hanging around and every twenty minutes or so the warehouseman appeared and handed a small wooden box to one of them, who then went on his way.'

'With a barrow empty except for a small wooden box?'

'Sorry, I meant to say. Each barrow was full.'

'With what?'

'Each barrow, there were ten in all, carried timber, as if it had not long arrived at the docks. Will assumed that it must be a timber warehouse that your nephew is employed in.'

'Will assumed! Did this Will not see inside the warehouse?'

'No.'

'Did Will not wonder what was in the small boxes?'

'I don't think so, no.'

'James, do you think Will might not be the sharpest knife in the drawer?' The Quartermaster shuffled some papers on his desk while awaiting an answer, but none came. He looked up at the Sergeant. 'On your way out tell the Sergeant of the Guard I wish a word.'

'But, I was going to have…'

'That's all James.'

#

The Sergeant of the Guard smiled as he entered the room.

'Sandy, are you a sight for sore eyes.'

'Was he not up to the task Sir? We did have our doubts.'

'James recommended that I give the lad a chance, but I'm afraid Will wasn't up to it. Do you happen to know this "Will"?'

'I do, it's James's brother Sir. I suppose the extra pay came in handy.'

It was the Quartermaster's turn to smile. 'You know what needs to be done Sandy.'

'I'll find out all you need to know soon enough Sir.'

'Good man.'

The Sergeant turned to leave.

'Sandy, a wee dram?'

He turned back. 'If you don't mind Sir, I've things to catch up on.'

'Well blow me down McLeod, in all my years in the Guards I have never known a Scotsman refuse a dram.'

'Well just the one Sir,' said Sandy, taking the chair opposite his Quartermaster, 'I have important work to be getting on with.'

CHAPTER THIRTY-ONE
Monday 20th November

'What brings you to Dunfermline this morning Martha?'

'Robert is at George Lauder's store.'

'It's a fine shop. Is he buying you something nice?'

'Don't be daft Annie. Where would we get the money for something nice? How are you fairing since your landlord was taken to the Workhouse?'

'That was terribly sad. He was so angry but couldn't quite find the words to express it. They had to put him in one of those straight-jackets and it took two burly men to put him into their wagon.'

'Poor soul.'

'Aye. He'll not be needing your medicine now Martha.'

'No. What is happening about the rent?'

'The lawyers who deal with the letting of the place own it and have asked if I can clean their office and make them a wee cup of tea occasionally. They said if I do that they would see to the rent. I thought that was very nice of them.'

'Did they know your landlord well?'

'Oh aye.'

\#

'I thought our meeting went well, didn't you Robert?'

'I did George. The weavers are all fired up about the behaviour in the factories,' answered Robert.

George continued. 'Since time immemorial the wealthy have tried to squeeze every penny from their workers and now is no different. Though in the past there was less worry about the power of the written word as the population in general could not read. Back then they took their lessons from the images in the Kirk windows or the verbal instructions from the mouths of their Masters.'

Robert sat down on a wooden crate. 'If you don't mind me asking, have you always been so concerned about the plight of the poor George?'

'Interestingly I have. I seem to be blessed with the ability to see things through the eyes of others Robert and I do consider it a blessing. Many men in my position can see only themselves and yet many of them can be seen in the Kirk on Sundays. They think that a few pennies in the poor-box is enough and their consciences are calmed. I find this very sad, very sad indeed. Tell me, is your master-plan complete?'

'It is George.'

'Should I call young George through to hear it?'

'Perhaps if we could share my idea beforehand. I do not wish to embarrass myself.'

'I'm sure you won't do that but we'll leave him to serve shop for the moment.'

'Build a library right in the centre of Dunfermline,' said Robert.

'A what?'

Robert looked straight at George. 'We build a library in Dunfermline.'

'Robert, please excuse my negativity, our sponsor is becoming wealthy but not to that degree and I certainly do not have the money to consider such a project.'

'Yes, I understand our position, but even the mention of a library and the creation of blueprints for that library may be enough to show our detractors that we mean business and will not see the people of Dunfermline reduced to mere fodder to feed their infernal machines and bank accounts.'

'Do you believe a blueprint and a hope could be enough Robert?'

'It may be possible,' answered Robert.

'A forlorn hope perhaps. I do not believe so much money can be raised nor how long it will take for your proposal to come to fruition. It may remain as a mere blueprint for eternity. Though I too have been thinking long and hard about the literacy problem faced by the weavers in the Pilmuir Works. The owners subject their workers to such long hours and in terrible conditions that it seems necessary that we do something more immediate.'

Robert stood up. 'We have tried by giving some of the weavers books but as was said at the meeting, that put their jobs under threat.'

'Nothing could be done to them if those books were only read in their homes.'

'They still have to get to the books or the books to them George.'

'Exactly my point. Didn't you once deliver books to folk's homes Robert?'

'Aye, but that was piecemeal, the occasional book to the occasional home.'

'What if you had a cartload of books, a covered wagon that went from house to house and handed out literature befitting our goal. That would get the weavers reading. It would also have the benefit of being accessible to their families.'

'I don't quite understand. Are you talking of a mobile library George?'

'Of course, but we would need a willing librarian. It would have to be someone we could trust and someone who knew the books cover to cover. Someone with a passion for literacy.'

'And where will we find such a man?'

'He would also have to be willing to distribute leaflets regarding our aims. It's a tall order and it may be necessary to sweeten our delivery of books with parcels of food for the readers from my shop, free of charge of course.'

'Whoever takes on that job would have their hands full. I think you may find it difficult to find the right person.'

'I am not so convinced. That man is sitting with me at the moment.'

'George, I cannot...'

'Robert, before you reject it out of hand, please think about it.. Discuss it with Martha and with your daughter. Remember this is only a mere stepping stone until we have our library. It will be a grand building of most intricate design and will hopefully be in the High Street. The people of Dunfermline and the ones you will be delivering your books to will come and go from the library, coming as the uninitiated and going as the learned.'

'So will we continue to pursue the planning for the building of such a place?'

'Oh yes Robert. You see our industrial, yet supposedly liberal culture, holds for inequalities and injustice which is presented to us as the fault of the poor, yet it is the very opposite. Literature, in all its forms, is part of a social movement where people's skills and knowledge are accepted as worthwhile to the whole of our society. Interestingly, the day after our last meeting I sent a message to our sponsor Andrew Carnegie and his immediate reply was that he had ambitions to see a library in Dunfermline and that one day this would happen. He too believes that education, particularly literacy education, is the tool to create a better and fairer society.'

'I have always believed that myself George.' Robert stood. 'I am sure that Martha and my daughter would be delighted if I accepted your position.'

'Of course there will be proper remuneration for such a demanding task, but for the moment I think young George needs to hear all we have to say.'

CHAPTER THIRTY-TWO
Wednesday 22nd November

Sandy McLeod smiled as he followed the man pushing a barrow along the quayside. 'Barrow boy,' he whispered to himself, 'that's a laugh. Will's "barrow boy" must be over six foot- three with a back and shoulders as broad as his barrow.' He approached the man. 'Excuse me son. Is this the way to Buckingham Palace?'

As the barrow boy turned to answer he felt a pain on his forehead seconds before falling onto the handle of his barrow then to the hard, cold cobbles of the road.

'You've not lost your touch Sergeant McLeod,' said the Corporal walking up behind Sandy. 'I still wouldn't go in the ring with you.'

'Now now Corporal Evans, you surely wouldn't back off from an old-timer Sergeant? I'll soon be joining the Yeomen Wardens at the Tower of London.'

'If we are caught out here tonight we could all end up in the Tower.'

'Trust a Welshman to be a feerdie. You should have thought about joining the Welsh Guards Evans.'

'I did Sergeant but you Scots needed me more.' Whilst Evans was Scots Guards through and through, he knew his Sergeant well so knew his comment was made in jest, just inter-regimental Guards Banter, but Sgt McLeod was not one to argue with so he let the comment ride with only a gentle riposte, despite also being a Welshman through and through.

The barrow boy moaned just as the other six men of the regiment appeared. Sandy leaned over the side of the barrow, lifted out a small wooden box and opened it in front of the men. 'Anyone for some opium lads? I think it's time we headed back to that warehouse, don't you. There is a young lad in there who might have got himself into a wee bit of bother. You get on your way sharpish. I'll have another word with the barrow boy here.' Before he did so Sandy walked over to the water's edge and threw the box over the side.

When the men got to the warehouse they saw the warehouseman handing out another small box to one of his men. 'Wait until their chief goes back inside lads,' ordered the Corporal, 'before we do what we came for.'

'Are we not going to wait for Sergeant McLeod?'

'I can read your mind Guardsman Balder. You are thinking that your Corporal here cannot function without his Sergeant, am I right.'

Before the Guardsman could deny his lack of faith in his Corporal their Sergeant appeared. 'He was a hard lad that.'

'I don't see a mark on you,' mused the Corporal.

'No, I mean when he hit that lamppost, I thought it would fall into the Thames.'

The soldiers' laughter was heard by the other thugs who turned around in unison.

'Looks like the fight is about to come to us lads,' said the Sergeant, stepping in front of his men.

What happened next was over within two minutes. 'You might have left one or two for us Sargeant McLeod,' said the Corporal as he winked at his men.

'Compliments will get you the promotion you deserve Corporal Evans, particularly after tonight's show, but I'm afraid the first prize must go to Guardsman Watt. Did you see him put that barrow boy down?'

'Sorry, I was too busy to notice.'

'Corporal, if you are ever going to be a Sergeant you will have to grow eyes in the back of that head of yours. Now if you'll excuse me lads I'm away to see a man about a boy.'

Just as Sandy was approaching the warehouse door, it opened and the warehouseman came out. He looked around before spotting his battered and bleeding gang on the cobbles. 'What in Heaven's name has happened to you lot!'

'I happened,' answered Sandy, leaning on the door, 'and the same thing is about to happen to you.'

The man immediately turned tail and tried to get back through the warehouse door but Sandy's large hand grabbed the back of his collar and pulled him over until he was on the cobbles. 'Sorry lad, but you won't be seeing the inside of that warehouse again, if you know what's good for you.' He twisted the man's collar until he could hardly breathe. In fact this is the last time you will be in this street or on these docks.'

'He can't breathe Sergeant!'

The Sergeant paid no heed to his Corporal and continued applying the pressure. It was only as his victim was about to go unconscious that he let go, lifted him to his feet and pushed him hard against the door of the warehouse. 'In case you do not comprehend my Scottish accent let me repeat my orders.'

After repeating his orders word for word the Sergeant pushed the man on his way then turned to his Corporal. 'Do you know of any welcoming inns down these parts Evans?'

'Oh aye, I do.'

'I thought you might. Right, get your motley crew in line, we're going for a drink.'

\#

Thomas waited for the noise to die down, all except the quiet moaning and groaning he could hear outside, and stepped out onto the street. He had his cane sword drawn but it seemed there would be no need for it.

Looking around for the warehouseman he saw the cause of the noises, but there was no sign of their boss. Apart from the bodies prostrate on the cobbles and the occasional moan there was no sign of anyone. He walked along the quay and looked at the ships docked there, wondering if the Captain of one of those had come for his revenge for not being paid.

As turned again towards the warehouse he caught sight of the warehouseman. He was leaning heavily against a lamp-post and looked as if he was struggling to breathe. Thomas still had his sword in his hand as he approached the man.

'Please Thomas, don't.'

'I'm sorry, I don't understand. What's going on?'

'I should have known, you understand it all.'

Thomas lifted the rapier to put it in its cane, causing the man to lean back sharply and fall onto a ship's capstan. He stumbled back to his feet and began shuffling away.

'It's all yours Thomas, all yours. I don't know who the hell you are but I'm having nothing more to do with you or your opium.'

Thomas headed back towards the warehouse and could see the warehouseman's thugs stagger to their feet and begin moving in the opposite direction.

He moved to follow them then stopped and turned into the warehouse. After closing and locking the door he walked to the back room of the place and checked the cargo that had newly arrived from India. He shook his head as he thought of the damage such shipments were doing in China and now here in London and on what had to be done.

For one moment he thought of burning the whole place down and took a box of matches from his pocket, but before he struck the match he sat down on one of the crates and looked around the dark chamber.

CHAPTER THIRTY-THREE
Sunday 12nd May 1872

Dalgety Kirk was busier than usual and the Petersons merely put this down to the fine May weather. Bluebells filled the forest floor and as they made their way home Mary picked a bunch to brighten up their dark cottage.

'One moment Peterson!' It was The Master's Factor.

For one second Mary thought she was about to be hauled over the coals for picking his flowers but the man made straight for her father.

'A word Peterson, if you please.'

Robert stopped and turned. 'What can I do for you Factor?'

'It's not for me the doing needs done. It's for the Master. He's asked me to have a word.'

'What about?' asked Robert, thinking he knew full well what was coming. The Factor's answer confirmed his thoughts.

'It has come to the attention of the Master that you have involved yourself with George Lauder and his son and that you are taking a horse and wagon around the area and giving out books and such like.'

'If you don't mind me being inquisitive, what do you think my relationship with George Lauder has to do with the Master?'

'You forget that you are still his tenant Peterson, though not good for much else. What you choose to do in these parts reflects on our Master.'

'Is there something about those books that displeases our Master?'

'What pleases, or displeases our Master is not for you to question. I have been told to inform you that if you do not do as instructed he may have cause to evict you from your cottage.'

'And what may I ask is my Master's instruction?'

The Factor looked as though he was about to choke on his next words. 'He wishes you to start a school for his workers and their bairns.'

'Pardon Hamish, what about my work with George Lauder?'

'The Master wishes you to start a school for his workers and their bairns.'

Robert put his hand behind his ear. 'You'll have to speak up, I can't quite hear you.'

'You heard me alright Peterson. The Master wants your Mary to teach in the school. He says that though home taught she is a very intelligent young woman and would make a good teacher. But I know different of course.'

'So the George Lauder announcement was all yours Hamish? The Master never spoke of it!'

'All I can say is that I wouldn't have your daughter teach my bairns, you'd never know what she'd teach them.'

'I heard that all right Hamish.' Robert Peterson punched the Factor so suddenly and so hard he fell over backwards to the dusty ground. 'If I ever hear another word come out of that mouth of yours regarding my Mary again, it will be the last word you utter. Now take yourself off and you can tell our Master that the Petersons would be delighted to see to his Lordship's school.'

Robert's womenfolk turned as he walked up behind them. 'What's happened to Hamish?'

'The poor man has an awful trouble with the drink. Did you not smell it in the kirk? We were blethering away when he suddenly fell over. I tried to help him to his feet but you know how stubborn he can be and insisted on getting up of his own accord. Anyway, we'd better get ourselves away home, that roast mutton will be about ready. I can tell you more of what he said then.'

129

CHAPTER THIRTY-FOUR
Wednesday 5th June

Journal 5th June

It would be ill of me to say that I am enjoying my new role but the result certainly cheers my heart and tonight I took another shipment of that wonderous plant into my warehouse.

The crew of the ship who delivered the last cargo seemed oblivious as to the contents of those crates and cheerily deposited them where I designated them to be put.

After Deciding not to put the place to the flames on that evening at the warehouse I took ownership of the place and its contents. When I returned home that night I thought long and hard about what my future would hold and yes my mind turned to destroying it all but I am now glad I did not.

Although never really one for alcohol I decided, before retiring, to have a sherry. I knew that Iain had kept some so searched his desk drawer for a key to his drinks cabinet. When I opened the cabinet to my surprise I saw, amongst the decanters and glasses, a large leather bound ledger. After pouring myself a large sherry I retired to an armchair, ledger in hand.

On opening the book I saw immediately what it contained - it was the names and addresses of all those who were receiving Iain's mind numbing goods. The list included the weight and cost of each delivery. It was then and only then that I made up my mind not to destroy that dreadful storeroom and its contents but to put those contents to much better use.

Had I not discovered Iain's ledger I would have had no way of knowing all of my customers, only those I am familiar with through my trading opium on the Stock Exchange and my contact in the East India Company.

Since that evening I have been taking delivery of shipments and personally supplying the opium in portions befitting the wealth of the recipients, of which there are many. I have carried out all deliveries disguised as a barrow boy.

I make sure that my cargo is paid for on delivery and because of that I now have merchants who approach me with offers of more affordable products.

Eighty percent of my profit is given anonymously to the Charities Society to enable it to carry out its good works. I am sad that I no longer have time to volunteer on the streets with them but am sure the amount of finance supplied by me will more than make up for my absence.

I believe poetic justice has now been served for all those poor souls who lost their lives to Algernon and Iain and their evil ways.

The other twenty percent of my profit is being saved by me for one day I intend to make the journey home and make an honest woman of Mary Peterson.

Until that day comes I shall continue with my work at the Stock Exchange and the supply of happiness to those unfortunate wrecks who cannot see past their wealth and fame.

CHAPTER THIRTY-FIVE
Monday 14th July 1873

The Petersons' year passed uneventfully. Their main priority, setting up the Master's school in one of the Master's outbuildings. It had been carried out by Robert and Mary with precision. They then spent many evenings studying and developing a curriculum that would attract and inform the children of the miners, farmworkers and salt-panners.

Martha continued to ridicule their efforts but to no avail, leaving the two educationalists to believe that she was merely hiding the fact that she was very proud of their achievements.

Yet no word had come from Thomas since Robert's visit and he had no idea if the Viscount had visited him after they'd spoken. The only proof that Thomas remained alive was the Savings Bank account which continued to grow, with larger and larger sums being deposited on a monthly basis. Though occasionally checking the account, Mary refused to withdraw and funds.

George Lauder's enterprise, to enlighten the weavers of the Pilmuir Works through works of literature, was working well. The threat of intimidation by the mill owners had come to nothing in the end. At one point those same owners had asked for a meeting with George where they congratulated him on his endeavours and offered financial support should it be required.

It took Robert some time to persuade George and his son that their offer was indeed genuine but eventually the two men accepted his interpretation of the offer. They did not however agree to accept any remuneration from the owners of the dark, satanic mills, as young George Junior called them.

July brought festivities season on Fordom, with colliery brass bands in abundance. Fetes, flower competitions and dances raised the normally dismal atmosphere of the place to a new height.

The Master himself put in many an appearance and supplied much of the alcoholic sustenance for the events.

The Petersons were preparing to attend a flower arranging event and had just closed their front door when the local postman came up the path.

'Not working today surely Peter.'

'The mail never stops Robert and I've one for you; you have mail from across the water.'

'From abroad?'

The postman smiled and handed him the letter. 'No, it's from Leith.'

'That will be from our son. We've not had a chance to visit William for some time. He's a hard working lad that, still at the weaving but it is wire he is weaving for the factories and ships of Leith.'

'We were at the free school together in Dunfermline.'

'I'd forgotten that Peter. Do you want a wee refreshment before you go?'

'I've post to deliver yet to the Big House before I can call it a day so I'll not on this occasion Robert.'

'Well you'd better get on your way. Maybe the Mistress will give you a refreshment.'

'Aye, she just might, then she might not. Maybe if I was a gardener.'

As the postman walked away Robert opened the letter and began reading.

'Well are you not going to tell us what is in William's letter husband?'

He continued reading quietly before folding the letter and putting it in his jacket pocket. 'We'd better be getting on to the show before the miners' wives sabotage your offering Martha.'

Martha knew by instinct not to ask anymore, particularly in front of Mary, and Mary knew by instinct not to question her mother's silence.

CHAPTER THIRTY-SIX
Tuesday 15th July

William's letter had said all they needed to know. Christine's mental health had improved when they took custody of Mary's child but that change had been temporary and for the past two months she had been acting completely out of character and no longer wished to speak to, or interact with, Thomas or William. To make matters worse William had lost his job at the wire works due to a lack of orders for the new product and he had taken to laying cobbles on the roads of Leith. This work paid very little and they could no longer pay their way. By the time William was home in the evening he was too exhausted to make up for the lack of attention to Thomas by Christine.

\#

When Robert and Mary walked into George Lauder's shop and apologised that Robert would not be able to do his rounds with the books that day and explained why, George not only insisted that he take the rest of that week off work but also that his son George take them to William's house in Leith in his horse-drawn carriage.

\#

When Robert and Mary climbed the spiral stair to the top of the tenement in Baltic Street they were unsure what they would find. William's letter had taken four days to travel the distance to Fordom and they both knew a lot could happen in that time. Robert was panting heavily when they got to the landing and he leaned over with his hands on his legs for support. Mary hammered on the door until it was opened by Christine who stared at them both but said nothing.

Mary nudged her aside and walked into the hall. 'Where is he?'

When no answer was forthcoming she marched into the living room-cum-kitchen. What she saw made her stomach churn and tears ran down her face. The whole room was filthy and a grubby china-sink at the window was full of dirty crockery over which the torn window drapes clung damp and forlorn. The sound of buzzing flies filled the air and in the centre of the scene sat the grandson of Viscount Havington; master of all he surveyed. Mary bent down, picked up her son and walked to the door. Without a word she passed Christine and her father and headed down the hard, cold stairs.

Robert stepped towards Christine. 'Will you be all right lass? When is William home?'

She did not answer but merely put her hand to the door and closed it, leaving Robert staring at the painted and varnished grain of the wood.

CHAPTER THIRTY-SEVEN
Monday 11th August

Completely oblivious to what was taking place back home on the Fordom Estate, Thomas Havington carried on in the business of procuring opium through the East India Company and selling it to the gentlemen, and occasionally ladies, of London. He was pleased with himself in that he saw much of his profit help many of the deserving and the undeserving poor rise from the gutters and sewers of the same city.

He chose not to dwell on the subject of what his wares were doing amongst the middle and upper classes, preferring instead for them to remain all but anonymous other than as a delivery address.

Unfortunately for Thomas this philosophy was not shared by one particular customer who became more and more fascinated by the barrow boy who delivered his goods. At first Thomas wondered whether the gentleman had more than a liking for young men but that was only until he saw him arm in arm with a very fine young lady.

Normally when he was delivering the gentleman's consignment, Thomas would hand over the small box, take the pouch of coins offered and be on his way, but all that changed as he arrived at the man's door with yet another consignment. Before he could hand over the box the same young woman he'd seen on the man's arm in the street leaned over the shoulder of her companion in the doorway and beckoned Thomas to come into the house for one moment as she had something to give him.

Not knowing what to do and not wishing to be rude he agreed and was shown through to the drawing room. After being led to a gold satin covered Chesterfield couch, one very much like the one in his father's drawing room, she insisted he sit down.

'Now Thomas, would you care for a small sherry, or is whisky more to your liking?'

Hearing the sound of his name he tried to stand up but a strong hand from behind him pressed down on his shoulder and held him in place.

'Please be careful John. Thomas is very special company, isn't that right My Lord?'

He thought about resisting but realised that it was pointless. 'How do you know my name?'

'We know all there is to know about you, don't we John. My brother Albert works in the Stock Exchange and he has taken a great interest in your, shall we say, clandestine buying and selling arrangements. Albert worked alongside your friend Iain and was so very sad to hear of his demise. He told me that it affected you terribly until a year ago or more, when suddenly your demeanour changed considerably and you began asking Albert questions about your friend Iain's dealing with the East India Company. Since then it appears that you have become the life and soul of Capel Court which, according to my brother, is completely out of character. So once Albert drew this to our attention we made it our business to follow you and low and behold, you are our barrow boy. But that is not all you are, is it My Lord?' You are the sole owner of an opium business that is making you rich, very rich indeed. I wonder what your father the Viscount would have to say about that?'

Thomas pushed hard against the weight of the man's hand. 'What do you want from me?'

The man removed his hand and came around from behind the couch. 'Silly boy, we want everything but perhaps we'll start with the keys to your warehouse at Executioners Quay.'

Thomas stood up and faced his antagonist. He was two inches taller than the man though more slightly built.

'Are you wishing you had your walking cane with you? Yes, we saw that too on your sojourns around our hovels. But it wouldn't do you much good here. You see, unlike your Edinburgh acquaintances I am proficient with the rapier and if you look at the wall there above the fire-place you will see my pride and joy. Now, can we get down to business, the keys!'

Thomas put his hand into his coat pocket and handed over the large iron key.

'Thank you. Now I don't think we have any more business to attend to,' he turned to the woman, 'do you darling?'

'I don't think so John, but we didn't give Thomas his libation.'

'Somehow I think the lad may have lost his thirst, don't you? Perhaps you'd better see him to the door.'

CHAPTER THIRTY-EIGHT
Tuesday 12th August

Thomas remained awake until three o'clock. His midnight oil being the sense of anger and revenge which flooded through his veins.

It was not until his eyelids began to droop that he came up with his answer. It was something his father had repeated time and time again when he was growing up and had dreams of becoming a warrior like his ancestors before him. 'Always remember son, the pen is mightier than the sword.'

As he became a teenager he grew to hate that phrase, believing that his father was merely a coward and had given up on the military because of that cowardice. If, at that time, he'd bothered to ask anyone who'd served with his father what he was like as a soldier they might have painted an entirely different picture.

That picture may have resembled the one Captain Havington's superiors had of him, the one which in the end caused them to be somewhat relieved when he chose to leave the regiment. Captain Havington fought like his father, Lieutenant General Havington but without his father's sense of fairness.

During the Crimean campaign it had come to the regiment's attention via Russian prisoners that what they feared the most in battle was any British troops who were led by the likes of Captain Havington.

Some British officers believed that it was his lack of fair play that had caused him to put so much energy into freeing his subordinate Private Walker from a murder charge. But Thomas knew none of this and still believed his father to be a coward. It was that supposed cowardice which, he believed, had caused his father to continually tell him that "the pen is mightier than the sword."

\#

When he awoke, the first thing he did was go to the bureau and make sure there was a sufficient supply of paper and ink. The second thing was to get dressed and visit the Stock Exchange and let them know that he would not be in attendance that day or any day in the future.

Before leaving the building he climbed the stairs to the first landing and went to his usual place. Albert was sitting only feet away. 'Good morning Albert.'

'Good morning Thomas, you're looking somewhat tired this morning; not a night on the tiles I hope?'

'No, not at all. I visited a friend up in Mayfair and yes, I may have extended my welcome somewhat and couldn't get to sleep when I got home.'

'That will not do. There's quite a bit of movement on the China front. This Dungan revolt is causing the stock to plunge sharply and making investors very jittery.'

'Opium,' answered Thomas.

'What?'

'The Tongzhi Emperor of the Qing Dynasty is attempting to modernise the country and opium is his nemesis, or one of them.'

'Where have you learned all this?'

'I've had a good Scottish education Albert and it has served me well. But I mustn't dally; I have a great many things to attend to today.'

'You are not here to work?'

'No, I have resigned.' Thomas lifted the lid of his desk and put his belongings into the carpet bag he was carrying. 'Farewell Albert.'

#

After visiting his favourite coffee house Thomas headed home and without further ado dropped the carpet bag onto the rug and went to the bureau.

The first letter he wrote was in his normal hand but the sender's name and address were not his own and neither was the signature. He wrote this letter to the Captain of the brig that at this moment was moored opposite the warehouse on Executioners Quay. The letter was allegedly sent by Sir John Quant, the gentleman he'd delivered the opium to the evening before.

It expressed Sir John's pleasure in taking ownership of the warehouse business from its previous owner and an apology for late payment of the last shipment. There was an invitation to the Captain to visit Sir John at his home this very night, where he would be entertained and paid in full.

The letter expressed Sir John's enthusiasm for the venture and how he looked forward to introducing the Captain to his lovely companion.

When he finished writing Thomas put the letter aside and placed another sheet of vellum on the red leather surface of the bureau.

My Dear Father,

Firstly let me apologise profusely for the way I have treated you and for my sudden departure from my home.

I know this letter is long overdue. For some time I have been wanting to write but only now have found the courage.

Fordom has and will always be my home and I now wish to return and take up my role as your son and heir.

Of course I will understand, after the way I have treated you, if you cannot find it in your heart to accept my return.

'I can only promise that should you accept me I will be a loyal, gracious and obedient servant to you and your causes.

Yours sincerely
Thomas
#

After taking his father's letter to the post-office Thomas headed towards Executioners Quay and the brig Ocean Mist.

The Captain was standing at the top of the gangplank watching his crew clean and prepare his ship. He was a big man and from his facial scars and wounds looked as though he'd seen more than his share of action.

'Good afternoon Thomas, is that you bringing my pay? The men will be pleased; they have been stuck on board since we arrived and have a thirst. Isn't that right men, Thomas here has brought your pay.'

A cheer went up from the crew.

'Well not exactly Captain, but I have brought you good news.' He handed the man the letter. 'I have sold my business to the gentleman who wrote you this letter. He is a man of great means and has spoken of expanding his contract with you. He has now taken control and full ownership of your last cargo and has informed me that you can go to his home where you will be paid in full.'

'Do you hear that my lads? Thomas here has not our pay but has a promise in this letter that we will be paid this evening.' The Captain held the letter above his head and waved it in the air. A grumble arose from the crew. 'Now now lads, we won't have any more of that. The first mate and I will be collecting your pay this night so you will have to hold your thirst until we return. I am sure your inns and whore houses can wait until then.' He turned to Thomas. 'And woe betide the writer of this letter if he does not have our pay.'

#

Thomas's next stop was a warehouse one hundred yards from what had recently been his own. The storeman was there as always and was happy to supply him with his request for two pots of brine and a sack of lime. He was also happy to barrow the products along to what he thought was still Thomas's warehouse.

Thomas produced the spare key he'd had made weeks before and shook the man's hand. Once inside the room at the back of the building he poured the lime into the brine and poured the mixture over the opium. He'd learned from his studies of the opium trade at Humen that in a short while the opium would turn to a scalding soup like substance and be of no use to the consumer.

As he locked and left the warehouse he wandered over to the quayside and threw the key into the Thames.

CHAPTER THIRTY-NINE
Wednesday 20th August

'Alice, we've had a letter from Thomas, he wishes to come home.'

'We've had a letter, that's nice. Can I see it?'

'Well actually it is addressed to me.'

'Now there's a surprise. And what does your blessed son want?'

'He wishes to come home to take his place at my side.'

'Don't you mean to inherit the estate, your estate?'

'Now Alice, we have had this discussion many times, he is my only son and rightful heir.'

'And I am your wife and I do not like the boy.'

'That has been very obvious since you arrived here.'

A servant knocked once and entered the drawing room with their afternoon tea. They waited until he had gone.

'Have you told your father the Earl of your dislike of my son?'

'I didn't have to; he saw Thomas enough before the rascal abandoned you. I believe he thinks him too much like his mother.'

'Did the Earl actually say that?'

'My father is a man of few words but I could tell he was not enamoured of your son, especially after he fathered a child to that servant girl.'

'Alice, I have replied to Thomas.'

'Is he to remain in London?'

'No, on the contrary. I have instructed him to come north as soon as possible.'

'George, how many times have I told you I do not wish to be in the same house as that boy. He is selfish and hot-headed and will cause us nothing but trouble. Look what he did the night before he left. That caused no end of trouble with the miners' families when he handed that gift to the gardener. Thomas has no concept of how difficult is the task of running an estate.'

'I was coming to that Alice.'

'What?'

'Running an estate, which is exactly what I am attempting to do, yet I am being undermined by the very one who should be my support. And that is you Alice. I would like you to leave this house today and I do not wish to see you again. Should you go to your father do not attempt to place the blame for this on me, or my son.'

'You are forgetting that my father is an Earl and you a mere Viscount. He can make things very difficult for you.'

'Not as difficult as for you my dear, should he discover what it is you have been doing in your beloved garden here at Fordom.'

Alice's face reddened but she did not reply immediately. When she did it was with venom. 'Has that servant girl been talking!'

'Oh, you mean our school-teacher? No, but my loyal and obedient cook has. She has been with my family since she was a girl and she could not bear to see what was happening to me, nor to this family. She told me that nearly everyone in Fordom knows of your disloyalty. I have known for some time but did not want to believe her. I am a friend of your father's so will keep this sordid business to myself but if you so much as try to blacken the name of this family I will have no option but to inform the Earl. Knowing your father as I do, I believe that may have a detrimental effect on your future legacy.'

Not knowing what else to say, Alice turned and walked to the door.

'Oh you can tell your father from me that if he is looking for a good gardener John Cant is well trained and is looking for work as of now.'

CHAPTER FORTY
Thursday 21st August

On the same day that Thomas put paid to the opium stocks, he vacated the house near Capel Court and moved into Brown's Hotel in Mayfair.

From there it was only a short walk to Sir John Quant's home and Thomas was in position nearby by six in the evening.

The Captain and the First Mate arrived just before seven and pulled on the brass bell. It was the lady who opened the door and Thomas could see quite clearly that no introductions were given as the two men barged their way into the house. They were there less than an hour before they reappeared, both carrying a large holdall in each hand.

#

The owners of Brown's Hotel, Mr and Mrs Ford, took Thomas to their hearts and as this was one of the few hotels in London to have a dining-room he was treated daily to the most wonderful fayre. They would bring his morning newspaper to the dining-room as he sat at breakfast and enquire as to his health and comfort.

It was Mrs Brown who placed the newspaper beside him on the table.

SIR JOHN QUANT AND HIS FRIEND LADY PENELOPY SPENCER FOUND DEAD AT HIS HOME IN MAYFAIR

'I see you've spotted the headline Thomas,' said Mrs Brown. 'London can be such a terrible place. When are you leaving for home?'

Thomas was quiet for some time before answering. 'I will be taking the Edinburgh train on Saturday.'

'Then you must have supper with us on Friday evening before you leave and you can tell us all about your stay in London and about your beautiful country. Mr Brown and I have never been to Scotland but he has promised me we will go to Edinburgh once we've retired.'

'Edinburgh is very beautiful Mrs Brown. I went to school there.'

CHAPTER FORTY-ONE
Wednesday 7th September

'William, is Christine with you?'

'She's in the hospital Pa.'

'Poor lass, at least she'll get help there son.'

'It's Gladstone's Women's Hospital for the Incurables Pa. I took her to Leith Hospital to try to find help for her but they tried to send her to the workhouse so I left and took her across the street to Gladstone's Hospital. They have taken her in.'

'Oh son, come away in to the fire. I'm glad you've come home. Your mother will be too. She is at the school doing some cleaning. She has the bairn with her.'

'Is Mary all right?'

'Mary is doing just grand and is teaching every day now. She's a bright lass and spends her evenings brushing up on her subjects. Thomas Havington has come home.'

'What! Should I have a word with him Pa?'

'Now, there'll be none of your shenanigans William, the lad is alright.'

'What, are you a friend of the Havingtons now father? You have come up in the world.'

'That I have, but not with the Havingtons. I am still working with George Lauder too, delivering literature around the area.'

'Well I never. Is he paying you for this?'

'Oh aye. What are you going to do now that Christine in hospital son?'

Just as Robert asked this the cottage door opened and wee Thomas ran headlong into his grandfather. 'I've been to the school. Mummy said I can go there when I'm big.' It was only then he saw William that he ran behind his grandfather.

'What's wrong Thomas?' asked Martha as she entered the cottage behind her grandson. 'Your step-father has come to see you all the way from Leith.'

Robert took hold of her hand. 'William has come home Martha. Christine is in a hospital for women in Leith. She is very ill and may never be released.'

Martha looked to her son. 'Is it the workhouse?'

'No mother. It is a hospital for incurable diseases.'

'Oh William, I am so sorry.'

'It's all right mother, it's for the best. Now what about you young man?' William leaned forward and took hold of Thomas and lifted him above his head.

'Let me go, let me go!'

He handed him to Martha. 'It would seem he prefers the company of the older generation.'

'He's got good taste the lad,' said Robert, causing them to laugh, all except Thomas who broke free and kicked William in the shin.

'You wee bugger!'

'Now William you're not in Leith now. Come on Thomas, granny will take you into the garden to pick some flowers for your mother.'

CHAPTER FORTY-TWO
Saturday 18th October

September moved swiftly into October for the Petersons. William had filled the gap in the Master's workforce left by the sudden departure of John Cant the gardener, but was assured by the Viscount that this was a temporary position until a proper gardener could be found the following Spring.

The abundance of trees on the estate meant there was no shortage of work for the ex-weaver. When he read the note sent down by the Master regarding his priorities his first thought was to ask for a rise in pay.

As well as stocking the wood piles for winter, the glasshouses, all three hundred yards of them, had to be scrubbed from top to bottom and the compost for the fruiting vines cleaned out. All the flower beds in the walled garden had to be pruned and weeded and all remaining fruits and vegetables given to Cook to prepare for conserving.

William and the cook got on well, she having known him since he was knee high to a grasshopper as she liked to tell him. Such friendly terms had its benefits for William when each day he appeared at the back door of the kitchen and collected his sandwiches, which she'd made up from the Havington's previous evening's meal.

He learned quickly that he could confide in Cook and what he said would go no further. This was reciprocated and William learned things that he could never have imagined about her life. Though he did admit that the biggest eye-opener was not from

Cook's own life but that of the Mistress and John Cant the gardener. 'Horny buggers gardeners' was how she put it.

'I hope you're not referring to me!' was William's retort. This was met by a handful of flour over his head.

#

As it was a Saturday, Robert thought he would take advantage of the fact that the Pilmuir weavers would finish work earlier than normal.

After loading his cart with the boxes of books that had been bought and paid for by George Lauder and Andrew Carnegie his sponsor, Robert went to look for William, in the hope that his son may want to escort him around the weavers' cottages.

When he found him in the walled garden William was up to his neck in weeds and twigs. 'Good afternoon Pa, what can I do for you?'

'Oh it's nothing son, I was just checking up that you were actually working. Word has it you spend more time in the kitchen than in the garden. Your mother actually asked me the other day whether the Master had given you a job as Cook's assistant.'

'And what did you tell her?'

'I said that might suit you down to the ground with the amount of food you eat.'

'Aye right Pa.'

'Did you ever read that book I gave you on Queen Victoria's visit to Edinburgh?'

'No, not had time yet.'

'There's a lot to learn in literature you know.'

'Not again father, please. Keep it for the weavers who need it. I'm happy as I am.'

'Well, I'd better get on my way, or those weavers will be chapping at the bit. I've books to deliver before sunset.' Robert began walking away.

'Did you ever get any bother from the mill owners Pa?'

He turned. 'Not a bit son. I think we were all caught up in the romance of it all. They've been fine.'

'That's good, but you will tell me if anyone gives you grief?'

'Of course son, but there's no need to worry about me, I can look after myself.'

#

'Oh, it's you Robert, come away in. I've been waiting for another book. I finished Thomas Paine's Rights of Man. I love the quote "The mind once enlightened cannot again become dark." It inspires me to read more.'

'And from what I hear, to do more too.'

'You've heard?'

Oh aye. It came to the attention of George Lauder's son in a local inn. You are starting a weavers' union.'

'I am that.'

'What are your new employers saying about it?'

'That is the interesting thing; they are saying very little Robert. When I told the foreman of my plan to unionise his workforce he merely said he would speak with the managers. When he came back to me he said that what I did in my own time was my business and that I could only speak with the workers in their own time too.'

'I don't know what's come over the managers Frank but I suppose stranger things have happened. Anyway, I've a whole box of books to deliver so I'd better get a shifty on. If you give me your book I'll see what I can follow it up with. I'll be back in a moment.'

Robert returned to the cart and leaned into the box on the tailboard. He knew what he was looking for and put his hand on it immediately; John Stuart Mill, On Liberty. As he pulled it from the box he felt a sudden sharp pain in the back of his knee, forcing him to buckle to the ground. Before he could turn his body, a blow hit him on the back of the head and threw him forward face first into the iron rim of the wheel.

The next thing he knew, Frank was bending over him and wiping his face with a damp cloth. 'Robert, what in Heaven's name happened to you?'

'I don't know Frank. I was just getting your book from the box and someone hit me hard behind the knee then hit my head with something very hard and heavy.'

Frank looked around but could see no-one.

'You'd better get me to my feet, I've more deliveries to do.' He handed Frank his blood-stained book.

'You'll not be doing any deliveries today Robert. I will be taking you home when I can get you onto that cart. I think you must see a doctor; your face is in a bad state.'

Robert began shaking uncontrollably. 'Perhaps the mill owners have been biding their time.'

'Perhaps they have Robert, perhaps they have.'

'Frank, you must promise me one thing, you will not tell William.'

'It's the furthest thing from my mind. What are you going to tell him?'

'I tripped and took a tumble against the cart and you saw it and came to my rescue.'

'Don't worry, your secret is safe with me.'

#

'Robert, what has happened to you?' Martha rushed towards her husband as he clung to Frank.

Frank answered for him. 'He's had a fall Mrs Peterson.'

'A fall! He'd need to have fallen off Ben Nevis to receive an injury like that.' She took hold of Robert and guided him to the armchair.

'He went to get my book and I saw him fall by the cart.'

154

Martha had stop listening to Frank and was looking to her husband. 'Perhaps you'd better get William. He's in the walled garden. And Mary too, she's preparing the schoolhouse for Monday.'

'I'll see to that Mrs Peterson.'

Frank went to the walled garden first, to look for William. When he found him he was bent double tugging at a weed.

'Will, your Mam sent me, your father has been injured.'

William immediately let go of the weed and stood faster than Frank had ever seen a man move. 'What's happened Frank?'

'He fell.'

'What happened Frank? I'll not ask you again.'

He remained silent, but only for a moment. 'Someone beat him.'

Without another word William headed out of the garden towards the cottage.

'Will, I promised your father I wouldn't tell you.'

Robert's son paid him no heed as he strode towards the cottage.

'I know who is responsible Will.'

William turned. 'Who?'

'Come to the Dunsmuir factory on Monday morning; they are looking for weavers. If you can get into the building I will point out the manager who takes care of those things for the owners.'

'Are you sure I will be able to gain entry?'

'Come early before nine. He will want to show you around if he is interested in employing you.'

'Are you sure that he is the same manager who did this to my father?'

'It is Will, of that you can be assured.'

CHAPTER FORTY-THREE
Sunday 19th October

The Peterson family did not go to the Kirk this day. On Martha's insistence Robert remained in bed, though he argued that she kept him from his prayers simply because she did not want the congregation believing that she had given him a pummelling.

Mary had gone up to the schoolhouse after breakfast as she had some preparation to complete for the following day's class. She was there no more than half an hour when her classroom door opened. She thought it might be William with the flowers she'd requested from the garden, but it wasn't.

Facing her was the boy, now man, she had not seen in nearly four years. 'Good morning Mary.'

'Good morning is it? You say it as if we'd met yesterday. After four years away with hardly a word you tell me it's a good morning. You have been home since August and never a word. You would have as well been in London, if that is where you were all the time you were gone. And what of young Thomas your son, you have not seen him.'

'Mary, I am sorry. I wante…'

'Well, just don't bother yourself. It would seem that I am always the last thing on your mind Thomas Havington. Your son and I can get along very nicely without you.'

'I have been speaking at length with my father.'

'I do not doubt that you have. And hiding yourself away in his house.'

'We had much to talk about.'

156

'Thomas, I am sorry but I must get on with my preparation for tomorrow's class.'

'Mary, will you do me the honour of marrying me?'

The chalk she'd been wielding fell to the floor just as William appeared with the flowers.

CHAPTER FORTY-FOUR
Monday 20th October

When Mary had returned from her preparations in the schoolhouse the day before, she was in a very jocular frame of mind. She carried a small bunch of flowers which she gave to her mother and a hand-made card to her father on which she'd glued a strand of grass and inside had written a poem.

Four years have passed;
Four summers, with the length
Of four long winters! and once again I hear
The waters, rolling from their mountain-springs
With a soft inland murmur.—Once again
Do I behold these steep and lofty cliffs,
That on a wild secluded scene impress
Thoughts of more deep seclusion; and connect
The landscape with the quiet of the sky.

'Mary, that is a beautiful poem.'
'I have plagiarised it somewhat father.'
He smiled. 'William Wordsworth, Lines Composed a Few Miles Above Tintern Abbey.'
'I knew that you would know the poem. It's my favourite.'
'And one of mine too. "While with an eye made quiet by the power of harmony, and the deep power of joy, We see into the life of things".'
'How are you father?'
'I am recovering darling.'

'And you mother?'

'Much the same as I was a wee while ago before you left for the schoolhouse. Though looking after you pair and this wee bundle of energy and now William is no easy feat.' Young Thomas was delving into the unlit stove as his Nana spoke and was covered in soot.

'I don't think Cook will be overjoyed if he delves into her stove like that.' suggested Mary.

'What are you talking about deary. Is William going to be taking him to see Cook?'

'No mother. Thomas Havington has asked me to marry him and if father agrees to this arrangement young Thomas there will be living in the Big House.'

Martha collapsed onto a small stool whilst Robert's smile broadened, causing a pain to shoot through his injured face to his forehead.

The remainder of that day had been spent talking about weddings, causing William to spend most of the Sunday afternoon in the forest.

#

On this day William rose at 4am and by six-thirty was striding out towards Dunfermline and the Dunsmuir Works. Frank had reminded him to be there before nine but William couldn't wait that long and decided to be there for eight.

As he walked through the large doors of the mill he was stopped in his tracks by a tall, thin beanpole of a man. He wore a bowler hat and black-framed spectacles. 'And what can we do for you lad?'

'I heard you are hiring weavers.'

'You heard right. What is your experience?'

'I have worked a home loom but never a steam loom, but I learn quickly.

'No doubt I'm sure. You're a big lad eh. Where did you get those muscles?'

'I took to timber work up Dunblane way when the handloom weaving died.'

'Aye, suicide really. These steam looms are the future,' he pointed and swept his arm indicating the extent of the mill.'

That's when William spotted Frank and got the nod that he was speaking to the right manager. 'So I've heard.'

'You know son lads like you can always pick up other forms of work and I'm in the business of hiring the likes of you. What's your name?'

'Willie, Willie Stevenson.'

'Willie, how would you like to be away from the looms and have a more lucrative employment?'

'I don't know what you mean? I'm a weaver.'

'If you can meet me at twelve noon at the Stag's Heid in the High Street I can tell you all about it? I'm a bit busy just now.'

'Aye, that should be all right.'

'I'll be buying you a bite of lunch and a jug of ale. Got to keep those muscles in fine trim.'

As William left the mill he glanced over to Frank who gave a subtle wink of the eye.

The time until twelve noon passed quickly enough. William had spent the morning at Annie's drinking the tea she'd requisitioned from the office she cleaned.

He gave her all the news he could of the family, all except the wedding news, but he was sworn to secrecy regarding the marriage of Mary Peterson to the future Viscount Masterton. It would perhaps be more fitting to say that he was threatened by Mary, beyond an inch of his life, not to utter one word on the subject.

#

By twelve noon William was leaning on the window sill of the ale house and could see the manager, escorted by two other gentlemen walk up the High Street towards him.

'Punctuality Willie, that's what I like to see. These are the men you'll be working with. This is Tam, and this is Brian.'

William shook hands with them both.

The manager turned to step into the inn. 'You've not shaken my hand yet Willie but perhaps that can wait till you hear what it is I have to offer.'

By the time they'd finished sharing a large venison pie and drinking their ale the four men were in a jolly mood. William had learned all about the clandestine business of the manager, paid for by the mill owners. To his complete surprise he learned exactly what had taken place outside Frank's cottage on the Saturday. He also learned that George Lauder's occupation, that of educating the weavers, was the mill owners' biggest gripe and made George, his son and William's father, their greatest enemies.

As they were leaving the establishment William turned and walked back to the bar, where he purchased a pint bottle of ale. He placed it in his jacket pocket.

'A bit of a drouth on you Willie. Ye'd better be sober for tomorrow evening. Come to the mill for 7pm. You start work then and will be given your instructions.'

As they walked along the High Street, William spotted a narrow lane just by the cobblers. 'One second gents, nature calls.'

'Aye a good idea that,' said the manager. 'We'll join you.'

As he followed William into the lane the beer bottle hit him squarely in the face, causing him to throw both hands to the injury. A severe kick to his groin followed and then a blow to his head in quick succession. His companions were so taken aback by the swiftness of the attack they froze to the spot. That was their first but not their last mistake.

And it was not the only fight they would have on their hands that day. The whirlwind that ensued in the lane that afternoon saw the three of them on their way to Edinburgh's Infirmary and by mid-afternoon, fighting for their lives.

#

To William's surprise the beer bottle had not broken and as he walked the miles home to Fordom, with hardly a mark on him, he pulled it from his pocket and studied the thickness of the glass, before tugging at the cork and taking a mighty gulp.

CHAPTER FORTY-FIVE
Tuesday 21st October

'George there was no need for you both to come and see me. I am recovering well from my fall.'

'A fall indeed Robert, you've gone down with some clatter.' George Lauder Senior walked up to Robert's armchair and took hold of his arm. 'It's been a time for accidents around Dunfermline.'

He put down his book. 'Why, what's happened?'

'One of Dunsmuir's managers and two of his cronies were found very badly injured in a lane near my shop.'

'What happened to them?'

'I'm not sure Robert. Some say they'd been drinking and carrying on and had a fall.'

'All three of them? They must have been carrying on. What day did it happen?'

'Just yesterday. Folk falling all over the place. Anyway, how are you?'

'Mending slowly and being treated better than before. If I'd known Martha could look after a man this well I might have become invalided sooner.'

Martha looked up from filling the stove but said nothing.

'I miss my darling wife dearly,' said George.

'Oh, sorry George.'

'It's been a while but there's not a day passes when I don't think of my Seaton. She was a lovely woman.'

'And a good mother,' added George Junior.

Martha stood from her toil. 'I'll just light this fire. A cup of tea and some fruit loaf gentlemen?'

'That would be very nice Martha.' replied George senior, 'it should not be too long before the servants will be making your tea.'

'Word travels fast in these parts George. We only found out on Sunday.'

'It most certainly does. Perhaps Cook has something to do with that?'

'And maybe that lad of mine too. Will you and your son be coming to the wedding George? You will be receiving a formal invitation.'

'That will depend Martha. Young George here is going off to America to join his cousin Andrew. It seems Andrew has a need of George's knowledge of steel. Isn't that right son.'

'It would appear so. Andrew's business is flourishing but there remains scientific problems with smelting and other area of the process.'

'You're a very clever lad George, said Robert. 'You'll be missed at the university in Glasgow and here in Fife.'

'I'll return as often as I can. I did ask father if he wished to come to the land of the free but he said he has work to do here freeing the weavers.'

'Aye, he's right there.' Robert sat fully upright. 'George there's something I wish to discuss.'

'Plenty time for that Robert.'

'No, it needs to be said now. I am giving up delivering the books. I'm getting too old.'

'Why don't we wait until you are better?'

'My decision has nothing to do with this injury. It has to do with my age and my general health. At times I struggle for breath.'

'Well if you are sure.' George turned to his son and spoke loud enough for them all to hear. 'Do you think this might be to do with Robert becoming father of a Lady my son?'

'Mm, we must think further on that Papa.'

'Are you sure you two scallywags want some cake?' exclaimed Martha and they all laughed simultaneously.

'You know Martha,' said Robert when the laughter had subsided, 'I would expect nothing less from that pair, especially the father. 'Did you know he wants to start a college for folk to learn handucation and headucation.'

'What in Heaven's name is that?'

'Don't ask me, the man responsible stands before you.'

\#

Father and son Lauder were almost at the edges of Dunfermline when the father asked. 'What am I to do now that Robert can no longer deliver our books George? He was perfect for the job and put his heart into it.'

'Loyal sons do the same, put their hearts into all they do.'

'Why do you say that George? I know you are loyal.'

'Robert has a willing and loyal son too.'

'Of course he does, if we can keep him out of prison long enough.'

'And I can guarantee that no thugs will prevent his deliveries reaching their intended readers.'

CHAPTER FORTY-SIX
Saturday 6th June 1874

It had taken week upon week of discussion between the Petersons and the Havingtons as to where to hold the wedding of Mary and Thomas.

The Petersons, particularly Martha, wanted it held in their church in Dalgety Bay but the Master continued to insist that it should be held in their private chapel.

Martha saw this as the Master merely wanting to hide the Petersons away and the fact that his son was marrying beneath him. Robert insisted that it was nothing of the sort to do with that kind of privacy. He believed that it was Havington tradition to be on the estate and in their private chapel for such a momentous occasion. 'After all, they were marrying into the Petersons and creating a very powerful future dynasty.' was how he put it.

'It is a crypt and no chapel!' Martha emphasised, on more than one occasion.

Robert was becoming impatient with his wife's deprecation. 'The Master has assured us that the estate will be open to all for the wedding and there will be a fete in the gardens afterwards. He has invited the miners and their families as well as all the estate workers. What more do you want woman?'

'A proper church wedding.'

'But the Dalgety minister is doing the service.'

'That's only because he is in the service of the Master.'

'Och, it's no wonder that mothers of brides have to wear the colour of mourning at their marriage. You are losing a daughter but you are not letting her go lightly. The day is about Thomas and Mary, and young Thomas here. Can you not just let it be?'

'Not on your life Robert Peterson. Not on your life.'

As she said this Robert coughed loudly, causing Martha to deeply regret her last words.

CHAPTER FORTY-SEVEN
Saturday 13th June

The coach arrived for Mary and her parents at 10am. It was pulled by two tall black stallions each of which had a different coloured plume on the top of its mane, one white to represent the bride and one black in honour of her father.

The coachman, who Robert knew well, was in his finest light blue coloured livery.

'Good morning Harry.'

Harry looked to Robert but was very obviously under strict order to not be in communication with his passengers.

William was last to leave the cottage and closed and locked the door.'

'There's enough room up here for the four of us son.'

'You're all right Pa, I'll enjoy the walk on this fine day.'

As the coach pulled away Robert thought that perhaps it should be William in a black gown as he appeared to be in more mourning than his mother. He knew his son would be thinking on Christine his wife, what might have been and what was.

\#

John the Gardener's widow Annie may not have been proficient with plants but what she didn't know about horticulture she more than made up for with her skills in dressmaking. Before meeting John she'd worked in her parents' bridal shop on the High Street in Kirkcaldy where they both taught her all the skills she would require to take over the shop. But all of that was before the young gardener crossed her path and from that moment she had not lifted needle nor thread other than to repair his work clothes.

When Martha approached her and told her of her daughter's marriage and asked the favour of her making the wedding dress Annie was more than reluctant until with her friend's persistence made her see sense and she agreed.

So when Mary stepped down from the wedding coach outside the Big House, Annie could not hold back her tears. The girl, as Annie stated over and over later, was beauty itself.

\#

At the end of the ceremony, when the Minister announced that the food and cake would be served on the lawn and warned the guests that by tradition he was to be first to taste Martha's home-baked wedding cake the proceedings lightened considerably.

By late morning the sun was at its height and broke through the trees as the guests made their way from the Chapel to the lawns of the Big House.

As they walked from the tree covered path into the open space of the gardens, Thomas looked around the crowd of miners and estate workers waiting there. Then he froze, becoming transfixed upon one man he had not set eyes on in some time and never outside of the London Stock Exchange.

CHAPTER FORTY-EIGHT
Tuesday 22nd September

Though he'd looked continually for Albert Spencer, his uninvited wedding guest, over the last three months, Thomas did not set eyes on him and had begun to believe that the apparition may have been nothing more than his imagination.

After the wedding Martha all but moved into the house to look after young Thomas, particularly as his parents were on honeymoon in Switzerland. To say that the weaver's wife immediately ruled the roost would not merely be an understatement, causing the Master to use expletives he normally only reserved for his unionised miners.

It wasn't so much personal insults to the Viscount himself that caused him so much grief but the regular complaints he was getting from his household staff regarding the unqualified, as they saw it, advice of Martha.

The one exception in somewhat negative opinions of the woman was Cook. She and Martha had hit it off right from the start and by autumn had become close and powerful allies. Their main enemy was the new Governess who began her employment on the day of the wedding and had moved in permanently to the Big House by the end of that day.

Recommended by an acquaintance from Edinburgh whose children had grown up and gone off to foreign parts, the Governess, though originally from London was, it would appear, well respected throughout the echelons of the upper-classes in London and Edinburgh.

Her references explained everything Thomas and Mary needed to know about Thomas's Governess, though none of the household staff knew her background. Cook's guess was that she had been a lady of the night but had given up due to lack of customers. Martha thought this hypothesis somewhat extreme and saw the Governess more as the daughter of a rich London family that had fallen on hard times. This did not, on the other hand, mean that Martha gave way to the younger lady's superior views and behaviours.

When orders came to the kitchen from the nursery regarding which particular food stuff would be best for young Thomas, the ladies always went out of their way to guarantee that such foodstuffs were not in supply.

At one point Cook had mentioned to Martha that she'd heard of her friend's abilities with herbal medicines and that maybe a healthy dose of one or other of those might warm the heart of the Governess. Martha declined on the basis that such medicines were nothing more than local fancy and did not exist in reality.

It was then that Cook attempted to raise the subject of old John the Gardener's wife Annie and her landlord's illness but her enquiries fell on deaf ears.

Conversations in the kitchen were mostly taken up by talk of the Governess and her strange ideas about healthy food for children. Eventually though the two older women put this down to nothing more than a modern fad.

The biggest advantage for Martha in her new relationship with Cook was that a meal hardly ever went to the Viscount without the same portion going to Robert at the cottage.

Everyone could see, not least Cook, that he was a changed man since his fall. He hardly ever left the confines of the cottage and when he did it was only for a short walk around the grounds.

It seemed to Martha that his only delight now was talking to William about his book deliveries and asking all about George

Lauder and his son. That was how he found out that George junior, though attending the wedding, would soon be leaving for America to join his cousin Andrew in the steel business.

It had been talked of for some time but Robert always thought father and son too close to let that happen. But leaving he was, and George senior would only have the company of his son for another week before he left for Glasgow and the ship that would take him across the Atlantic Ocean.

CHAPTER FORTY-NINE
Sunday 15th November

It was not until the ground was too hard to dig and the flowers had been seen their best that William was released from his gardening duties to attend study at the Botanical Gardens, Edinburgh.

He regretted having to give up the book deliveries but promised George Lauder that he would continue once home.

He had taken up lodgings not far from the site of the botanical gardens near the top of Leith Walk. His landlady was a friend of the Viscount and was happy to accommodate such a fine, strong young man as William.

Being a Sunday he thought it fitting to take a stroll down Leith Walk to the heart of Leith where he and Christine had lived and to visit her. The thoroughfare was busy as the weather was good for the time of year.

He stopped once or twice to gaze in the shop windows and it was whilst gazing into a tool machine shop that he heard the voice behind him.

'Well, if it isn't Willie Peterson. What brings you to Auld Reekie on this fine Sunday afternoon?'

'It's William to you John,' answered William seeing his reflection in the glass. He didn't turn around.

'Aye, sorry I forgot. You Petersons were always thinking highly of yourselves.'

William turned quickly. 'Maybe not quite as highly as you, John, what with Alice and such like.'

'I didn't marry her though William, did I.'

William moved quickly towards his antagonist who stepped back off the pavement onto the cobbles. 'You'd better watch out John or you might get run over.'

'Look William I was only making small talk.'

'Small talk indeed from a small man. Now let me get on with my day John, if you'd be so kind.' William turned back to look in the shop window.

When John Cant put his hand on his shoulder William was taken aback and turned again. 'What's this?'

'We got off on the wrong footing from the start and I want to apologise for that.'

'You're a wee bit late.'

'It was not of my making William. Alice wanted the gardens clear of everyone and did not want any of your family, particularly Mary, finding out about our little games. She told me to make sure you did not feel welcome anywhere near the garden or forest.'

'Alice? And how is Lady Masterton?'

'I've no idea. She returned to her father, the Earl Rathmore, after she left Fordom. She asked me to apply for a job as gardener there but I could not guarantee that Viscount Masterson would not tell the Earl what had occurred between us. I was left without work for some time until I found a job with the Church of Scotland in Edinburgh. The Viscount was kind enough to give me a reference, though God forbid I do not know why.'

'Because he is a kind man, John. He has welcomed my sister Mary to the family and treats her like a daughter. I have learned much recently.'

'How is Robert, your father?'

'He is unwell.'

'I would have liked to work with him. He is a very intelligent man and very kind but I could not get round my Mistress's wishes.'

174

'I'm not sure whether to believe that or not.'

'You can only take me at my word. Would you mind if we walked together? I am going to the Gladstones' Hospital; it's adjacent to Leith Hospital.'

'Why are you going there?'

'I have a sister who has been there for some months. Both my parents died in a rail accident a few years ago and there is only Margaret and me. She took consumption . The hospital is for women who are incurable.'

'I know that John.'

'How can you possibly know that?'

'My wife Christine is in the same hospital, I'm on my way there now to see her, but she won't recognise me; she has an illness which affects her brain.'

'William, I am so sorry. Did you and she not adopt Mary's bairn?'

'Not quite adopt. We had him here in Leith to stay with us but then Christine became too ill to look after him. He is now living in the Big House with his mother and father, and a doting Grandfather too.'

Both men turned at that and began walking together down Leith Walk. Suddenly William stopped.

'Is everything all right William?'

William put out his hand to shake John's. 'It's Will to you John.'

CHAPTER FIFTY
Friday 3rd December

'Would you look at what the cat's dragged in Martha, a wee boy and he has not eaten his porridge, look.'

Martha turned towards the kitchen door and there, still in his nightgown, was her grandson holding his bowl of porridge towards her. 'What are you doing here Thomas? You are not allowed in the kitchen, you know that. You'll get into trouble and you've not eaten your porridge. Does your Governess know you are here?'

'Don't like it.'

'But you always eat Cook's porridge.'

The boy walked straight up to Cook and handed her the bowl. 'Don't want it.'

Martha lifted him up. 'Where is your Governess Thomas?'

'Gone out.'

'Where?'

'She not coming back.'

'How do you know?'

'She filled her bag with clothes said she would never see me again.'

'How odd,' said Cook, still holding the bowl of porridge. 'Thomas are you sure you don't want this. You love Cook's porridge.'

He shook his head, looked down and pushed the bowl further away from him. 'Don't want it.'

Martha stood her grandson down onto his feet. She put her hand forward for the bowl. 'Let me have that Cook.'

'See, granny is going to feed you and you'll be fine.'

Martha did not take the spoon to Thomas's lips but put the tip of her pinkie finger onto the porridge then to her lips.'

'Does it taste all right Martha? I've not done anything different in the making of it.'

'No you haven't, it's maybe the oats? It's possible some aconite has found its way into the sack. These things happen all the time. Not to worry, I'll just wash out the bowl.' She moved quickly to the sink, poured out the porridge, making sure it was fully down the drain then washed the bowl thoroughly. 'Maybe we can give Thomas his favourite. Do you have any apple pie left?'

'That I do Martha. You sit yourself down son, and let Cook take care of you.' She put a slice of apple pie on the table.

'You'll both have to excuse me,' said Martha, I'd better check the nursery and see what's what before we tell the Master what has happened.' As she left the room she heard a conversation strike up between Cook and her grandson.

#

Once in the top floor room Martha closed and locked the door and began looking through the drawers and wardrobe for any sign of where the Governess may have gone. She knew why she'd gone in such a hurry, for she'd put wolfbane in Thomas's porridge and had he taken one mouthful he would now be writhing on the nursery floor in the agony of his death throes. The Governess knew that she'd have to be well away from Fordom before Thomas took that first bite and must have instructed him accordingly.

Martha continued looking around the room when she noticed a piece of paper sticking out from the protective cover of the desk. When she pulled it out it was the address of the Coaching Station

177

in Dunfermline. There was a timetable too and a time for the Edinburgh coach marked out clearly.

\#

'Cook, do you think you could look after Thomas for the day? You'll have to be discreet as he's not supposed to be in the kitchens.'

'Aye, it would be my pleasure Martha, eh Thomas.' The boy smiled broadly as he tucked into another slice of pie. 'Have you told the Master about the disappearance of the Governess?'

'No, I'd prefer if we kept the Governess's disappearance to ourselves for the moment. She might return.'

Cook looked to her charge. 'Aye, perhaps she will. Where is it you are off to?'

'I was thinking it's been a wee while since I've seen Annie in Dunfermline and she's been on my mind a lot.'

'Annie? Do give her my kindest regards, oh and give her this.' Cook went to the shelf and lifted down a ham.

\#

'Robert, I've had an awfiest notion to visit Annie in Dunfermline so I'm taking the day off.'

'Might I remind you dear wife that one can only take the day off if one has a job.'

'Now don't go on about that again. I'm looking after the bairn, as well you know.'

'What I know is that the bairn has a mother, a father and a Governess, that's what I know. I hardly see you now. You're never away from that Big House.'

'He has no Governess as of today. She has left without a word.'

'This morning?'

'This morning, early.'

'How strange. She seemed a nice enough lass when I met her on one of my wanderings in the forest.'

'Was she with Thomas?'

178

'No, she was picking flowers, aconites if memory serves me well.'

'I'd better be off if I'm going to see Annie.'

'I suppose if you've had one of your witches' premonitions it's for the best.'

'Now don't you start about that again Robert Peterson, or I'll be putting a spell on you! I'm just nipping out to the shed to see if I can find a tincture for the lass.'

'Why, is she ill?'

'Not as far as I know, just something to brighten her up.'

In the shed Martha lifted the floorboard she'd kept loose since they'd moved to Fordom and stretched her arm down into the damp space and brought up a metal box. When she opened it she saw that the same poisons she'd stored there for use in dire emergencies were still there. 'And this is one such,' she whispered to herself as she lifted the syringe and drew up the liquid from the small bottle marked Aconite.

She returned to the cottage. 'Robert, my dearest, it's a tall order, but you couldn't see your way to take me on the book-wagon to Dunfermline?'

'Oh, I still have my uses then?'

'On occasion. Do you feel up to it?'

'I might be old but I'm not an invalid yet.'

'Excellent. I'll get the hap off the wagon. I suppose you've had breakfast?'

'Thanks to your lovely daughter and her husband who brought me some ham and eggs.'

'You could always charm the birds off the trees Weaver. Could you harness up the horse?'

'Rocinante will have missed me. I haven't been out with him since that day.'

'I know husband, I know.'

#

Robert drew the wagon up adjacent to Annie's cottage and was about to step down when Martha put her hand on his arm.'

'I wish to visit her alone husband.'

'Women's stuff?'

'Aye.'

Rocinante gave a whinny as he too had been looking for a rest before the weary road back to Fordom.

'Gee up Rocinante, I know the very place where we will be looked after.'

#

Martha waited until Robert was out of sight before walking past Annie's cottage and up the steep slope to the centre of town. Wrapping her large shawl about her head so her face could not be seen she entered the yard of the Coaching Station and looked around at the people awaiting their coach to Edinburgh.

The fine young lady she was searching for was in plain sight standing near the front of the queue.

Taking on the gait of a woman much older than herself Martha shuffled up to her and nudged against her.

'Mind where you are going you silly old woman,' cried the Governess.'

Keeping her head bowed Martha apologised before shuffling on. She could not have been more than a few yards distant when she heard the young woman gasping for air, then falling to the ground.

'No-one shall touch one hair on the head of my grandson Thomas Peterson, not while I am alive,' she said to no-one in particular.

#

Albert had waited for his young sister for some time when the coach from Dunfermline eventually pulled to a halt at Edinburgh's Dean Bridge. He stepped forward to help her down but an elderly gentleman was the only one to exit. Albert leaned on the side of the door frame and peered in to the dark interior before turning to the alighted passenger.

'Excuse me Sir, but whilst in Dunfermline did you happen to see a young lady of fine stature with fair hair? She has the voice of a Londoner such as my own.'

'Did she carry a carpet bag of blue damask?'

'She did. I bought it her for her twenty-first birthday last year. She's my young sister.'

The elderly man stepped closer just as the coach drew away over the bridge. 'I am most terribly sorry.'

'It is of no import. She surely must have missed the coach.'

'Your sister is dead.'

Albert stared at the man for some time.

'She collapsed at the Coaching Station and could not be revived. It was perhaps food poisoning as she had the most terrible end. I am so sorry.'

Albert was already walking away then turned. 'Was there anyone with her?'

'No-one. The poor thing just collapsed immediately after an old woman mistakenly bumped against her. There was a doctor awaiting the coach and he attended her immediately but could find no blame for the onset of the spasms that soon took the poor girl.'

\#

By the time Albert returned to the house of Mrs Hyde, the widow of Algernon and mother of Iain her deceased son, he was the worst for wear. He'd very obviously been drinking and could barely stand.

His landlady appeared from the drawing room. 'Albert, is everything all right?'

'No.'

'What is it and where is your sister? Such a lovely girl.'

'My sister is dead. She has been murdered.'

181

'Oh Albert, come into the drawing room and tell me what has happened.'

'I will Mrs Hyde. I will tell you everything that has happened tomorrow morning.'

#

Martha had gone straight to the lawyers office from the Coaching Station, where she knew she would find her friend Annie at work. It was just gone lunchtime and Annie was about to finish for the day. 'Martha, what are you doing here?'

'I've come to see you.'

'Well you've come on the right day. Remember my landlord the weaver?'

'Aye, I do that Annie. He's a hard man to forget.'

'Well the poor man has gone and died.'

'The poor soul.'

'He tripped and fell in the asylum and never recovered.'

'And are you in mourning?'

'No, not quite. I was just speaking with his lawyer before you arrived. According to his lawyers, the ones I clean for, he has left me everything in his will and a very large sum of money.'

'Well I never.'

They said that as David and I were cohabitating, I think they called it, which is the same as marriage in Scots Law, that I had rights as his next of kin.'

'What lovely lawyers he had. But David didn't appear to be a saver Annie.'

'No, he wasn't. He spent most of his siller on beer, but a few years ago he was left a farm by his cousin and when he sold it he put the money in the bank and never touched it.'

'Well I never Annie dear, that certainly is worth celebrating. I think we've still time for lunch at the alehouse, don't you?'

'That we do Martha, that we do.'

CHAPTER FIFTY-ONE
Saturday 4th December

Albert appeared in Mrs Hyde's dining-room just after eight o'clock. His breakfast had been put under silver chafing dishes, though Mrs Hyde wasn't sure her guest would have any appetite after what he'd told her the night before.

'Albert, have you slept?'

'Not much.'

'Do you want any breakfast?'

'No thank you. Do you have coffee?'

'Of course. I'll get Daphne to bring a pot. I was so shocked to hear your news. Your sister was such a sweet girl and that was why I had no qualms about giving her that reference for George Havington. Please come through to the drawing room. We can talk better there.'

Albert took one of the armchairs by the fire and Mrs Hyde the other.

'How could this have happened to such a sweet girl? You said last evening that you had lots to tell me Albert. Do you feel like doing so now?'

'I do, and after I've told you perhaps we should go to the police.'

'That is a very good idea. How do you know she was murdered?'

Daphne entered with the coffee pot, causing Albert to withhold his answer until she had gone. When he did begin he told Mrs Hyde how he and her son Iain had become good friends whilst working in the Stock Exchange. He then told her everything he knew about Thomas Havington in relation to her husband Algernon and her son.

He chose his words well, indicating that it was Thomas who was trading in opium and it was that illicit trade which led to the death of her husband and son. He did not mention his older sister Lady Spencer nor her companion's involvement in the affair.

His sorry tale took some time in the telling, the conclusion being that Thomas Havington was a bad lot and had threatened poor Albert on the day he left the Exchange. That made him sure that somehow Thomas had discovered that his son's governess was Albert's sister and this had caused him to take revenge on her.

As he took his first sip of the by now cold coffee Mrs Hyde spoke for the first time since he'd begun his story.

'Albert, you obviously do not know how well I know the Havingtons. I would trust that family with my life. What you say cannot be as you have indicated and is an outright lie. You may wonder how I can possibly know this. Let me enlighten you.

After my husband and son's death and long before your arrival here, I had a visit from two Pinkerton detectives who told me a very different tale from the one that you have told. Those American gentlemen made it clear that it was my husband who was dealing in opium and it was he who had firstly encouraged my son and then poor Thomas to become involved.

My husband was a very bad lot Albert and though I was heartbroken to lose my son, I felt no such remorse for Algernon. When you came to my door with your sister and told me of your friendship with Iain I was more than happy to take you both in but after what you have just told me I believe the best thing would be for you to depart this house, but not before we have sent Daphne to get the police.'

Mrs Hyde leaned forward and lifted a bell from the hearth but before it rang out Albert lifted the poker from the hearth and struck her full force across the forehead.

As he was leaving the house Daphne appeared from the kitchen. 'Do you wish more coffee Albert?'

'No thank you Daphne. Oh and Daphne. Mrs Hyde is not feeling too well and is having a nap. Perhaps it's best if you leave her to rest. I'm just popping down into Stockbridge. I shan't be long.'

CHAPTER FIFTY-TWO
Sunday 5th December

Albert awoke to the sound of a cell door opening and jumped to his feet to confront a prison guard. 'Where the bloody hell am I?'

'Welcome to Calton Gaol laddie.'

'Calton Gaol!' He staggered back against the wooden bed as his legs gave way. He looked around him with disbelieving eyes.

'So you've heard of us in London then?'

'Who hasn't?'

'True. Jules Verne the French writer visited and thought our wee prison reminded him of a medieval town. Now here's your porridge, you'd better eat it up, it's all you'll be getting this day. He handed the bowl to Albert, who took one look at the sloppy mess and immediately placed the bowl on the wooden spars of the bed. 'How did I get here?'

'Do you not remember laddie? You were taken from the London train before it left Edinburgh and you resisted arrest. Not a very good idea with our constables. By the time you arrived here, you were unconscious.'

'Why was I arrested?'

'Something to do with a Mrs Hyde. Her maid did not do as instructed by you and the moment you left the house she checked on her mistress. She found her alive but at death's door and ran for a neighbour, a Dr Braithwaite, then to Stockbridge where she found a police constable and told him the story. The police put a watch on the station and the harbour in Leith and here you are.'

Albert tried to stifle a whimper then began to cry. 'This is not of my making.'

'Aye, that's what they all say in here son. Keep your stories for the judge and pray that Mrs Hyde survives or you will be hanging from a rope in this place. Even if the poor woman does survive she will no doubt have her story to tell and as she is a well-respected lady of Edinburgh society the judge will not take kindly to you coming from the south and using her hospitality before trying to kill her. You may have heard, we Scots take quite some exception to such disrespect.'

He tried to stand but his legs would not support his weight; he collapsed on the floor shivering. 'I'm cold.'

The warden lifted the bowl of porridge from the bed and poured its contents over his trembling body. 'That should warm you up lad, as long as the rats don't eat it first.' Then he took his wooden baton and poked Albert in the chest before hammering it hard on his knee and kicking him full in the ribs.

'I am charged with looking after you for the rest of this day son. Maybe you should make the most of it. My colleague Bruce starts tonight at six and he might be wanting a word with you. He doesn't much like the English our Bruce.'

CHAPTER FIFTY-THREE
Friday 26th March 1875

Aconites and snowdrops were in abundance in the glades of Fordom, much to the pleasure of Martha, who'd requested her grandson have the afternoon off from the schoolroom to escort her in collecting her specimens.

As she picked and placed the flowers in her trug Granny Peterson explained all there was to know about the property of the flowers, despite young Thomas's disinterest. He was more concerned with climbing trees and throwing stones at any piece of water he could find.

Martha smiled. 'Nothing changes Thomas. Your Uncle William did exactly the same at your age, never paid one minute's attention to your old granny. But I wasn't so old then and I could catch the wee blighter and give him what for.'

When his granny spoke Thomas always looked up from his endeavours, but only for a moment.

'If you don't pay attention I'll have you back in that classroom before you can catch a breath.'

'Yes Nana.'

#

Towards the end of the afternoon Martha and her charge returned to the classroom just as the other children were leaving. 'You're a sissy, going with your granny!' could be heard from many voices as the children ran into the yard.

'I told you mother he would suffer for having the afternoon off.'

'Aye, as maybe, but he has learned a lot more than those scallywags this afternoon.'

'Thank you very much. I do try.'

'I didn't mean that daughter, as well you know. How was your class?'

'Much the same as ever. The miners' children are keen to learn but most of their parents, both fathers and mothers, work down the mines and by the time they are home they do not have the energy to listen to what their bairns have been learning or to encourage them to stick in at school. If only they realised that by their children sticking in at school they may not end up with a life of drudgery and an early death from lung disease.'

'Like your father Mary?'

'I didn't mean that mother.'

'No, but you said it. Your father is not at all well now.'

'I know.'

'I wanted to speak to you and to your husband about that.'

'What about it?'

'It's the cottage. Robert is spending more time in there and the place is draughty and damp and not doing him any good.'

'What are you suggesting, that you move to the house?'

'Don't be facetious daughter. The Big House is not for the likes of your father, nor for me for that matter.'

'That's not what you said when Thomas asked you if you'd be his son's Nanny. Since then you've hardly been out of the place.'

'Well your son doesn't have a Governess. It made sense that I step up in her place. I don't think your son is objecting,' she turned to the boy, 'are you young man?'

'No Nana. I like having Nana looking after me Mummy.'

'There's no winning with you two. So what are you suggesting about the cottage, mother?'

'I had hoped you might find us a better cottage. The West Gatehouse has been empty for some time.'

189

'But that's a Georgian cottage with gardens with outbuildings.'

'Exactly, it's just what your father needs.'

'I'll have to have a word with Thomas; I cannot make decisions like that.'

'Why not? You are his wife and future Lady of the Manor.'

'Oh mother! I'll have a word with him when he returns.'

'Why, where is he?'

'You will not know the woman but he received a letter from a Mrs Hyde in Edinburgh. She wished to see him on a very important matter relating to her son, whom Thomas knew when he was at school in Edinburgh. Unfortunately the woman has lost Iain her son. It was he who helped Thomas find work at the Stock Exchange when he'd gone to London and I think she wants to hear all about their time there.'

'Could Iain not have told her about their time in London?'

'He didn't get home. He was killed, murdered to be exact.'

'Oh my goodness, you never said.'

'Thomas didn't want me to drag up his past any more than necessary. We don't talk about his time in London but he did agree to visit Mrs Hyde and that is where he is today.'

\#

Thomas and Mrs Hyde were about to be served afternoon tea by her maid Daphne. They sat in the same chairs as she'd sat with Albert the day he attempted to kill her.

In some strange way she felt sorry for Albert but the Edinburgh Magistrate hadn't and the young man would more than likely spend the rest of his life in Calton Gaol.

Mrs Hyde had Daphne deliver food parcels to Albert but she wasn't sure those parcels would ever reach him.

Once Daphne had wheeled the trolley of scones and cake into the drawing room she curtseyed to both Mrs Hyde and Thomas before taking her leave.

190

'Oh Daphne, I don't think I'll require your services again today. I'll see you tomorrow same time.'

Thomas waited for the servant to leave. 'Does your maid not live in?' he asked.

'No, I have given her a mews house just off India Place. You most likely passed it on your way from the coach stop. She shares it with my coachman Mark.'

Mrs Hyde poured the tea. 'Now come, tell me all about London and your time with my son Iain.'

Thomas had dreaded this moment, the moment when he would be confronted about his time in London. What he had not expected was that that moment would be with the wife and mother of the men he'd killed.

'There's not very much to tell really. Your son Iain was very helpful to me when we got to London and he found me a job in the Stock Exchange.'

'And my husband, Sir Algernon Hyde?'

'I didn't…'

'I think we'd better stop there, don't you?'

'Mrs Hyde, I am truly sorry for what…'

'You obviously didn't hear me, or perhaps you are a stubborn one like your father.'

'My father?'

'Of course, you wouldn't know.'

Thomas was becoming exceedingly uncomfortable. 'Wouldn't know what?'

'Many years ago your father and I loved each other very much but my father was such an old mule. Your father was much older than me and Papa thought him beneath me, even though he was to be a Viscount. But that was not enough for my upwardly thinking Papa.'

'I knew nothing of this.'

'No, I didn't expect you would. Anyway Papa's problems were solved when George went off to the army. Those were difficult times with Crimea and such like and I didn't hear from him for many months and by then my beloved father had found me a suitable match. Algernon was more my age and talked much of land and high hopes. He certainly had my father's ear, until that land in the Scottish Borders he'd bragged so much about turned out to be nothing more than a sheep pen and my father's hopes were dashed by Algernon on the first hurdle at Leith Races. But by then Algernon and I were married and living here in this house which had been given to me by an aunt. When your father returned from the war he went to see my father and no-one to this day knows exactly what went on but my wretched Papa was never the same again. He became the kindest, most loving parent any young woman could hope for.'

'My father went to see him! My father is a mild mannered writer of diaries and letters.'

'Thomas, your father is much more than that I can assure you. From what I have heard, from sources close to him, he was a bit of a swashbuckler.'

'That is not what I thought. I believe that he left the military because he couldn't suffer the company of soldiers and the violence of battle.'

Mrs Hyde laughed out loud. You must be careful making assumptions Thomas, especially about your father. Maybe you will learn the truth about him one day.'

By the time she'd finished telling Thomas all about her relationship and her love for his father it was getting on for six. 'Perhaps we have let Daphne go too soon. There is some cold pie and chicken in the kitchen. We can share supper in a little while, after I have finished telling you what you need to know about Algernon Hyde. Do you wish another refreshment?'

'No thank you Mrs Hyde.'

'Well I'll continue. Algernon was a gambler and spendthrift and as losses mounted he became more and more violent, not just to me but to our son Iain. If this house had not been in my name only he would have had it sold and spent the money.'

'Is that why your son called himself Iain Cockburn and not Hyde?' interrupted Thomas.

'Quite possibly, Cockburn is my maiden name. Things got so bad that at one point I thought of going to see your father but didn't as I was frightened of what your father would do to him. Anyway, the brute mastered over me and my poor boy and he did whatever was bade of him.' She took a sip of her cold tea. 'It was that which caused your problems in London. Iain wrote to me and told me everything about you and your work with the Charities Organisation. He felt such remorse dragging you into his father's schemes but had no choice. And now he is dead. Which I suppose brings us, you and me, to where we are now. Did you know that your acquaintance from the Stock Exchange, Albert, came here?' She didn't wait for an answer. 'He gave me his version of events in London during your time there, but his version was somewhat flawed when compared to that of Pinkerton's detectives.'

At the sound of that name Thomas all but fell from his chair. 'Two American gentlemen?'

'Yes, but don't worry, I had to know and was glad to know, even though I do miss Iain terribly. Unfortunately, when I gave the reference for Albert's sister to be your son's Governess I had no idea about any of this. Have you found out how she died?'

'The authorities found a vial of wolfbane in her travel bag and assumed that she either ingested it accidently or took her own life with it.'

'Poor girl.'

'Albert and his older sister and companion were attempting to blackmail me in London.'

'I thought as much. His older sister died too, didn't she?'

'Yes, murdered by the people she and her companion were hoping to do business with.'

'People you too had done business with, unless Pinkerton's men are mistaken?'

'They are not mistaken Mrs Hyde. There are things I must tell you.'

'Perhaps this is not the time, if there will ever be a time. You are tired young man, and it's a long way to Fordom. You can stay if you so wish?'

'Thank you, but I must be home tonight.'

'Well if you give me a moment I shall make you a supper for your journey.' For a moment she stared into space. I have never been there you know.'

'You are most welcome to visit Mrs Hyde. I am sure father would be more than happy to see you.'

'Perhaps one day, but I have something more important to ask of you before then. Does your son have a Godmother?'

'No, he doesn't.'

'Would you have any objection to me becoming his Godmother? You see Thomas, now that I have lost my son I have no one to leave my estate to and I could not think of anyone more fitting than a Havington, chiefly your son and my old love's grandson.'

'Mrs Hyde, under the circumstances I do not think it fitting and proper that I…'

'Circumstances change with the tide of time Thomas and we cannot know what the future holds, only that we must love first and question only when there is something to gain from it. Now I must get you that supper.'

#

As Thomas walked up India Place towards the coach stop at the Dean Bridge he had a deeply felt sense of relief and began smiling to himself. At that same moment he felt his feet leave the ground and he was being propelled forward by two men, each holding an arm.

'Put me down or I will..'

'What Thomas? What will you do?' The two Americans dropped him gently back onto his feet.

'I will call the police.'

'We are the police and here at the request of both our Government and yours.'

'What do you want with me?'

'Nothing very much. Only the contents of your Bank of Scotland Opium account. Oh of course, it's not called that, is it?'

'I cannot believe this. I am being robbed on an Edinburgh street by two American detectives.'

One of the men produced a pistol. 'Would gunpoint make it easier Mr Havington?'

'Don't listen to my colleague Thomas, he can be a bit hot headed. We are here because we are charged by our Government to do two things. Firstly we have to remove the fatal flaw from your alibi. That is your bank account. If it ever came to the attention of the authorities just how much money you were depositing while in London you would not survive the scrutiny. Secondly, we need to know more about the new opium markets opening up in Britain and are therefore more able to impact on and have more chance of preventing the same thing happening in America. The funds from your bank account will help Pinkerton's achieve this end. Once you have transferred that account over to Pinkerton's it will be used solely for drug prevention work. We are sure that this will sit well with your conscience. Your friend Iain told us all about you and how you were roped in against your will. Then there is your charity work whilst in London.'

'I don't understand how you know so much about me.'

'We have been keeping a close eye on you since we interviewed Iain and I must say, you keep some strange company. Wherever those men came from the night you went up against the warehouseman, my God, their leader was like a whirlwind. You know some powerful people Thomas. But I think we've said enough. We will let you ponder on what we have said and if you are in agreement we will meet with you at your bank on the Mound here in Edinburgh next Friday at ten. If you do not appear we will know your answer and you ours soon enough. Goodnight young man.'

CHAPTER FIFTY-FOUR
Saturday 27th March

Mary pulled aside the heavy curtains of their bedroom, allowing the morning light to bathe the room in its yellow hue.

Thomas had been asleep, though she had been awake half the night. 'What time is it Mary?'

'It's gone seven. You were home very late.'

He pushed back the quilt and threw his legs over the edge of the bed. I had to walk from Dunfermline. The coach almost lost a wheel in the darkness coming from Edinburgh and it took more than an hour to repair. By the time we got to Dunfermline the handsome cabs had stopped for the night.'

'Did you see Mrs Hyde?'

'I did. The woman is heartbroken about her son Iain.

'Poor woman.'

'But that was not all. Mrs Hyde and my father had a relationship when she was a mere girl. It only ended when he joined the army.'

'Well I never. He's a bit of a dark horse your father.'

'Mm.'

'Be that as it may you will have to go to see him on some very important business that has arisen in your absence.'

'What business? I have a very busy week ahead of me and do not have time.'

'As you know my father is unwell and getting worse.'

'I am sorry Mary. I greatly respect your father and he has given loyal service to our estate.'

'He has Thomas and to me and I believe it is time the estate returned that loyalty.'

'Is it not enough that I married his daughter?'

'Thomas Havingt…'

'Thomas leaned over, pulled her onto the bed and pinned her down.'

'I love you, weaver's daughter.'

'Get off me you brute!'

He lay back with his head on the pillow. 'What is it that can be done for your father?'

'He and mother should be moved into the West Gatehouse.'

'The West Gatehouse? I'm not sure what Papa will have to say about that.'

'There is only one way to find out, ask him. It has been lying empty for some time. I am not sure how much longer we may have my dear father with us but I wish to see him as comfortable as possible.'

'I understand Mary, but I am unsure whether Papa will. These things are more complicated than they seem.'

She put her arm about his chest. 'Thomas Havington, you are not the man I thought you were.'

'If you put it like that, I am sure I can talk him round but it must wait until the week after next.'

'Time waits for no man husband.'

CHAPTER FIFTY-FIVE
Monday 29th March

Thomas Havington looked at his reflection in the window of George Lauder's store in Dunfermline High Street.

He had still not spoken with his father about the Petersons moving into the West Gatehouse. The events described at Mrs Hyde's still haunted his waking moments and prevented him from thinking of anything other than Iain, his father and Pinkerton's men. That was why he was here at George Lauder's store. Apart from informing George of Robert's failing health, he wanted to ask the man for his son's address in America. Perhaps he could shine some light upon the dealings of Pinkerton's detectives and help ascertain the real reason behind their presence here and in London.

As he stared into the glass of the window he half expected to see the two detectives in the reflection but when he turned they were not there. What he saw in their stead was a burly, bearded soldier.

'Well if it isn't Thomas Havington of Fordom.'

'Do you know me Sir?'

'I do.'

'And may I ask how that can be? I certainly do not know you.'

'I have seen your portrait. You were younger when it was painted but you have not changed much.'

'And who might you be that you have seen my portrait?'

'I served with your father in Crimea and we met a few years later by chance here in Dunfermline and he showed me the locket.'

'He does have such a locket. What is your name?'

'Major Hector Walker at your service Sir.' The man stood to attention and saluted firmly.

'You say you served with my father in Crimea. He never speaks of his time with the regiment and never of war but spends his days writing letters and diaries.'

'Does that surprise you?'

'Quite frankly, yes it does. His father was a Lieutenant General in the regiment and a very brave man but my father shows little of his stature.'

Walker laughed loudly.

Thomas lifted his walking cane and part slid the rapier free. 'Do you mock me Sir?'

'No, I do not Thomas. Please accept my apology. Now if you would care to put that knitting needle back where it belongs, perhaps I can tell you all about your father.'

\#

Thomas and the Quartermaster spent the next hour in the only coffee house in Dunfermline talking at length about Thomas's father, particularly when he was in the military. By the time they left the premises, not only had they become good friends but the soldier had an open invitation to visit Fordom. He was also told that should he ever leave the regiment that there would always be a job for him on the estate.

As Thomas walked back the few yards to George Lauder's shop he had even more to think about as he watched the soldier disappear at pace westward. That man and he had something very much in common – both their lives had been saved by another and that was none other than his own father, the writer of diaries.

\#

'Father, there is something we need to discuss.'

'I am somewhat busy at the moment Thomas, can't it wait until tomorrow? I should be free tomorrow afternoon.'

'It is very important.'

'As is the correspondence I must write before we meet.'

'More important than me, your son?'

'It involves you, my son.'

'I do not understand.'

'I will be writing to a lady in Edinburgh. A lady I have not seen in many years, but a lady that you have visited recently. I received a letter from Agnes Hyde, nee Cockburn, this afternoon.'

'Papa I...'

'Our meeting can wait until tomorrow. I believe you have much to discuss.'

CHAPTER FIFTY-SIX
Tuesday 30th March

The Viscount was sitting behind his desk when Thomas entered. He stood and walked to greet his son before directing him to a wicker chair in the corner by the French window.

'This chair came from Crimea you know. I bought it from local tribes people who were selling them to passing armies. Now, what is it I can do for you my boy?'

'I couldn't tell you I would be meeting Mrs Hyde, but then I didn't know that you and she had been lovers Papa?'

'Would you have told me had you known? It was a long time ago.' The Viscount sat in the winged chair opposite Thomas.'

'It seems there are many things that happened long ago that I know little of but before I enquire about them there is something of a more urgent matter I must request.'

'What is that?' The Viscount pulled a bell cord by the side of his chair. 'Perhaps a sherry might ease the conversation.'

'I wish Mary's parents to be moved into the West Gatehouse.'

If Thomas had asked whether his father was going to work down his mines the older man could not have been more shocked. 'Thomas, have you lost your senses?'

'No father, I believe I have come to my senses. Robert Peterson is very ill and his ill-health stems directly from the work he did for our estate. You know as well as I do that the dust from weaving chokes the lungs and leads to pulmonary disease, the disease that Robert is now dying from.'

'No more so that the dust from our mines that makes our miners ill. Do you wish me to house my miners in the West Gatehouse, or maybe even our house?'

'Is that such a bad idea?'

The Viscount smiled. 'Perhaps we must discuss your future as head of the estate if that is how you envisage its future and your duties.'

A servant appeared. 'Caleb, some sherry please. The Amontillado I think.'

'Yes My Lord.' The servant left.

'I welcome that discussion father, after we have solved the Petersons' problem.'

'How do you think it will look to our other workers if we prioritise Robert's family over them. There are others on the estate with more pressing needs.'

'But they are not your son nor my father-in-law, nor are they the grandfather of my son. I am sorry Papa, but I must insist.'

The Viscount's smile broadened..

'Do you find this funny Papa?'

'No. I find it ironic, for that is exactly the position I would have taken when your age. We are very alike Thomas, though I suspect that is not how you see it, is it? Of course our weaver can have the Gatehouse.'

'Thank you Papa.'

The servant reappeared with a tray.

'If this conversation had been taking place a few days ago before I met Mrs Hyde and the soldier I would have agreed with your analysis of how alike we are, but all that has changed.'

'What soldier?'

'Major Hector Walker, we met in Dunfermline yesterday.'

'Walker! How is the rascal?'

'Very well from the look of him. He asks kindly after you and sends his best wishes. I have extended an open invitation for him to visit.'

'Good man Thomas. Is he on leave?'

'Compassionate leave; his Mama is very ill.'

'Oh, I am terribly sorry to hear that. Walker is a Dunfermline man, and a bloody good man.'

'One who is glad you were his immediate superior in Crimea?'

The Viscount lifted a sherry and handed it to his son. 'Is that what he told you?'

'He told me everything, and why you were forced to leave the regiment. He says that in an earlier time, the time of your father, you'd have been hailed a hero, just as your father had been. But things had changed by your time and conduct and fair play amongst the officer class had become the standard, even at the cost of their men's lives.'

'So you know why I left the service?'

'I do. I also know about your involvement in my situation in London.'

'Well you know more than me; Walker was sworn to secrecy.'

'It was my fault he opened up, not his. I made the mistake of being somewhat indiscrete about who I thought you were and he became agitated and could not hold his tongue.'

'He told you everything?'

'Everything, including London and your regiment. I did congratulate him on the quality of the hampers he left for me every evening on my doorstep. I thought they'd been delivered by my neighbour.'

The Viscount stood and walked towards his son. The two men clinked their sherry glasses together.

'Are you going to meet with Mrs Hyde father?'

'That is for me to know and you to find out my young whippersnapper.'

'Then perhaps we can discuss my future role on the estate?'

'We have been discussing it throughout the afternoon my son. I now know that I could not have a better man to take my place and run the estate and I am confident that your son, with Mary's help, will do the same.'

'Mrs Hyde dearly wants to be Thomas's Godmother.'

'I know, she told me in her correspondence. She hopes you will accept.'

'I had to speak with Mary first and she agrees.'

'That is all to the good. There is however one other important business to discuss.'

'What is that Papa?'

'What are we going to do about that infernal Nanny Martha?'

Both Havingtons laughed louder than they had in quite some time.

CHAPTER FIFTY-SEVEN
Friday 2nd April

Thomas deeply regretted that he could not be in attendance to supervise the Petersons' move to the West Gatehouse, but he had to be in Edinburgh early if he were to meet Pinkerton's men.

Mary could not understand why her husband would not be at the flitting, as he normally did his banking on Thursdays. 'Thomas, tell me again why you suddenly decided that you need to do your banking today? You were at the bank yesterday.'

He did not answer for some seconds as lying, benevolently or not, was not in his nature. 'As you are aware I have knowledge of the markets and when I saw in the newspapers yesterday that my shares are plummeting I am now forced to transfer my funds before they are decimated.'

'Is that why you must go to Edinburgh, to transfer your shares?'

'It is.'

'Well, if it is so important you'd better go, it's past six. Thankfully my brother William is here to help with the move.'

'And Papa has given two members of staff and a wagon for the afternoon. I am truly sorry Mary.'

'Well I suppose you did get them the house.'

'That has nothing to do with it as well you know. Now, I must dash. I will see you this evening.'

#

Thomas stepped down from the coach on Princes Street and walked up the Mound towards the bank. It was nearing 10am and he was about to sign over a very large sum of money to complete strangers.

George Lauder Junior had been helpful in his research into Pinkerton and it seemed they were what they said they were. He was surprised to learn that the agency was started by a Scot, Allan Pinkerton. He had been responsible for saving Abraham Lincoln's life and the President was indebted to him and had hired Pinkerton agents as his personal security during the Civil War.

It was that information which convinced Thomas that giving the account over to the agency was for the best, though he was about to ask for proof of contract and was not sure whether such a document would be forthcoming.

As he turned the corner he could see the two detectives waiting outside the bank. They seemed to be admiring the architecture. If only they knew that less than a hundred yards from where they stood, were the most rat-infested, tenement hovels.

'Good day gentlemen.'

'And to you young Sir. So you have made your decision?'

'Not quite. I must ask you for proof of this transaction before it can happen.'

'Oh, do you hear that Wilbur, the young man would like proof of this transaction.'

Wilbur put his hand into the inside pocket of his coat, causing Thomas to take a step back.

'Don't worry son, Wilbur keeps his pistol in his other pocket.'

Wilbur removed an envelope and handed it over to Thomas. 'I hope this will satisfy your requirements.'

Thomas opened the envelope and read the letter. It was headed, Commendation and was from the President of the United Colonies of America, Ulysses S. Grant. It went on to thank him for his work in fighting the terror of opium and his charitable works in working against the awful effects of that wicked poison. Thomas could hardly believe his eyes.

'Will that do Mr Havington?'

Thomas was speechless, but only for a moment. 'I believe we have some business to attend to inside gentlemen, don't you?'

#

When the three men exited the bank, escorted by the manager, they stopped and thanked the man before turning right and walking to the where they could view the entire north side of the city.

'It is a beautiful town you have here Thomas.'

'Yes, but Dunfermline is my town. It was once the capital of Scotland.'

Wilbur put out his hand to shake Thomas's. Then once more put his hand into his coat pocket and smiled as he produced a large box. We have been asked by our President to thank you personally and give you this.' He handed the heavy box to Thomas. 'Please do not open it here. Wait until you are on your homeward journey.' At that both men saluted the younger man. 'We have also been told to inform you that if you ever find yourself in America that Pinkertons would be delighted to offer you employment. Now, we must take our leave. Goodbye Thomas and good luck with your future.'

#

Thomas's coach was almost at Queensferry before he unclasped the lid and opened the box. He was looking at a Colt 45 revolver with a pearl handle and a note atop the barrel which read, Thank you Thomas, *Ulysses S. Grant.*

CHAPTER FIFTY-EIGHT
Sunday 4th April

The West Gatehouse was at the furthest reaches of the estate which meant that Robert needed a wheelchair to get him from the cottage to the Havington's private chapel for Sunday Service.

By the time they'd got halfway to the chapel, William was starting to regret volunteering for the job of pushing the chair. The roads of Fordom had not yet been tarred and the single wheel at the front of the vehicle was more inclined to find its way into the ruts of the path.

'You sound more breathless than I am son,' wheezed Robert. 'Mind you don't have me lying on the roadside.'

'Aye Pa.'

'Are you regretting not taking up Thomas's offer of the cab?'

'Not on your life.' William pushed harder at the slight to his manhood.'

'A horse would've made the journey without the need for heavy breathing.'

'Pa, for a man with hardly a breath in him you can fairly express yourself.'

'Aye.'

\#

Robert had expressed himself clearly enough the day before when their furniture was being moved into their new abode. He'd always been a stickler for everything in its place, particularly his chair as it had to be nearest the window to give him enough light to read from. But despite his interruptions all had gone according to plan and by dinner time they were settled and enjoying the larger space and light.

Martha insisted the removal men stay for some refreshments supplied by Cook, but being a Friday evening she could see they were anxious to be away to whichever establishment they frequented.

When they had gone William announced that he was going for a look around the gardens. Robert could see that his son was enjoying his new role as Fordom's Head Gardener.

When the door closed Martha looked over at her husband. He was in his chair and about to open the first page of Paradise Lost.

Her first thought when she studied him was, would he be here long enough to finish the book. Her second, would she want to be here alone, without her weaver.

CHAPTER FIFTY-NINE
Monday 1st May 1876

Seven year old Thomas held his Grandpapa Havington's hand tightly and looked on as his mother and father removed the framed panel from their bedroom wall. The clock hands had just turned nine.

They'd been at breakfast and were preparing for their busy day, all except young Thomas who awaited the company of his Nana Peterson, before he could head off to the mischiefs and mysteries that awaited him in the forest. But all that was before William arrived at the breakfast table to inform his sister that she'd better be at the West Gatehouse as soon as possible.

#

As the Havingtons made their way along the track that led to the cottage Thomas junior ran off into the mass of bluebells that covered the forest floor.

'If school was in the forest you'd never have any trouble getting this one to behave.'

'He's just a wee bit spirited Papa,' answered Mary.

'Just like his father,' answered the Viscount.

'And grandfather, from what I hear,' added Thomas.

Mary stepped from the path. 'Thomas, come and carry this panel for me. It's for your Nana.'

Mary knew that the sound of his beloved Nana's name would have her son charging back from his adventures. He stretched out his arms. 'Yes Mama'.

'Now be very careful not to drop it.'

'No Mama.' He held it tightly in both arms.

#

It was with a sense of trepidation that they arrived at the West Gatehouse. Mary would normally have walked straight in but faltered. Her knock was answered by William telling her to enter.

She stumbled over the threshold as her son barged past her and handed his Nana the panel. 'It's for you Nana.'

Martha placed it against the fireplace wall but did not answer.

'Are you alone daughter,' wheezed Robert.

'No father, I have the Viscount and my husband with me.'

'Well don't leave them out there in the cold.'

Mary turned and called them in. The Viscount walked straight to Robert's bedside and shook his hand. He didn't speak. Next in line was Thomas, his son-in-law.

Robert smiled. 'It's all right Gentlemen, I'm not dead yet.'

'And not for a while by the looks of you,' answered the Viscount before turning and walking over to Martha, indicating as he did so that they should move out of earshot of Robert. 'I hope you do not mind my being here Martha?'

'It's your house Sir.'

'Yes, but it's your home for as long as you wish it. How is he?'

'He'll not see the day out.'

'I am so terribly sorry. He is a fine gentleman, your husband.'

'Yes.'

'You must consider staying on here.'

'Thank you My Lord, but I'll have to see. My friend Annie has offered me a room in her cottage in Dunfermline when the time comes.'

'Could she not live here?'

'I dare say.'

'You'll remain looking after your grandson if you stay. You cannot travel from Dunfermline every day to do that.'

'I understand.'

'There is one other thing. I have another job for you.'

'And what might that be My Lord?'

'Curator of a fine museum.'

'I don't understand.'

'When I removed Robert's handloom from your cottage I had it restored. It is now back there and your old place has been prepared for visitors.'

'Sorry My Lord, but I am not at my best and cannot fathom what it is you are saying.'

'Martha, your husband was the finest damask weaver in all of Fife and a great many of my guests who have admired his workmanship will testify to that. But the days of the handloom weavers are numbered and I would like our future guests and local people to be able to have access to their story. I have had your old place made into a museum where Robert's work can be displayed and I wish you to be the curator. I have also asked Mary to include lessons about his work, for the children of our school.'

'Does Mary know about the museum?'

'It was she who insisted we keep it secret as she wanted to surprise you, but under these dreadful circumstances she now wants her father to know and for that reason you too must know.

Martha did not answer but turned to poke at the coals in fire.

'I must be going now Martha. I will say my farewells to your husband before I do.'

'Could you tell him about the museum My Lord?'

#

As the Viscount was leaving, a handsome cab drew up and two men stepped down.

'Good morning Lauder and to your son. What brings you back from the Colonies young Sir?'

'Good morning My Lord. My father and I had much to discuss.'

'I have heard tales of your adventures with Mr Carnegie.'

'Aye, a fine opportunity for engineering.'

'Well I'll not keep you, you've enough to be getting on with.'

'How is he?' asked George senior.

'Not good Lauder. You'd better go in.'

#

When Robert saw who had just entered the house he tried to sit up.

'Stay where you are weaver, my son has some things to tell you while I'm introducing myself to young Thomas here and seeing if Martha might make us a brew. It remains chilly out for the time of year.'

'Ne're cast a cloot till May's oot. You should know that George,' said Martha going to the stove for the pot of tea.

George introduced himself to the boy and after a moment of small talk sat in the armchair by the side of the fire.

'What is your son telling my husband George?'

'Something I only discovered when he arrived from America on Friday.'

'And what might that be?'

My adopted son, in all but name at least, Andrew Carnegie, has initiated the building of a library in Dunfermline and it will not be long before architects will be employed in drawing up the plans. All our hopes have come to fruition, in no small part thanks to your husband and his determination to have folk read.'

'Aye, he's always loved his books.'

'It is more than that Martha. Robert wanted people to access a world that only readers can access; a world of mystery and wonder, a world where we learn who we are and that we deserve better than what we have. The foundation stone of such a place, a place for reading, will be laid and we are going to propose a reading room in the library named after him. Andrew is also talking about funding a college in my name but that is further down the line.'

Just as George finished speaking a large cough echoed through the room. They both turned quickly and looked across to Robert. He was lying peacefully with his eyes closed and a broad smile on his face.

EPILOGUE

'Did you know Robert Peterson, Stevie?'

'I never met him but have heard much about him. He's got a surprisingly large and ornate gravestone for a man who was a mere weaver.'

'He was no mere weaver Stevie. Robert Peterson was a man amongst men, and women, and children. Now we'd better get on carving his name and whatever you do, do not make a mistake; he was a stickler for the written word.

THE END

HISTORICAL NOTES

Fordom Estate along with its inhabitants is fictional, though much of the history surrounding the events in this novel are real.

The damask handloom weavers of Fife were in abundance at the start of the nineteenth century but as the century wore on many of those involved in this intricate but hard toil lost their living with the introduction of the steam loom.

By the mid-century the Pilmuir Works in Dunfermline was producing enough damask to satisfy the needs of changing fashions and wealth.

It was in this maelstrom of conflicting loyalties, traditions and invention that the families of George Lauder and Andrew Carnegie lived and worked.

George Lauder, a shop-keeper and political activist, was related to Andrew Carnegie's mother and he took Andrew under his wing as he grew up. Consequently Andrew became a close friend of George's son George Lauder Junior. Little could the two boys know then that they would one day run one of the most successful steel businesses in America and that Andrew would become the richest man in the world.

George Lauder Senior's name would also be carved in stone when Andrew chose to fund a college, as well as a library, in Dunfermline and name the former the George Lauder College.

As for the handloom weavers of Fife, many remain confined to an unwritten history.

GLOSSARY
Scots – English Translation

Scots		English
A	-	I
ae	-	always
alane	-	alone
anywie	-	anyway
auld	-	elderly
aw	-	all
aye	-	yes
ba	-	ball
bam	-	stupid person
bairn	-	child
beat it	-	go away
blaw	-	blow
blether	-	conversation
braw	-	pretty
cannae	-	can not
cause	-	because
clamjamfry	-	a mob
clarty	-	dirty
claithes	-	clothes
cloot	-	cloth
cossies	-	road cobbles
daen	-	doing
daft	-	stupid person
dinnae	-	do not
eejit	-	stupid person
feardie	-	frightened person
floers	-	flowers
gaun	-	go or going
girn	-	to cry
glaikit	-	stupid
gonnae	-	going to

gowd	-	good
guid	-	good
haud yer wheesh	-	be quiet
heid	-	head
hings	-	hangs
huddie		haddock or stupid person
intae	-	into
Jambo	-	Hearts supporter
jammy	-	lucky
jani	-	janitor or concierge
laddies	-	boys
loup	-	leap
ma	-	my
Ma	-	mother
mankie	-	dirty
mair	-	more
masel	-	myself
na	-	no
nane	-	none
neep	-	turnip
o	-	of
oer	-	over
oot	-	out
piece		sandwich
playpiece	-	food for school children
polismen	-	policemen
sae	-	so
sair	-	sore
schoolbairns	-	schoolchildren
sodjers	-	soldiers
steamie		steam launderette
telt		told
thankit	-	be thankful

tattie	-	potato
tick	-	debt
tigged	-	to be resurrected by a touch
topped himself	-	committed suicide
whae	-	who
wid	-	would
widnae	-	would not
yin	-	one

Printed and bound by CPI Group (UK) Ltd, Croydon, CR0 4YY

06/01/2024

03650611-0001